Ohayo! It's summer in Tokyo and thirteen year old Jacob is not happy about it. But middle grade readers will be as they watch him struggle with the language, the culture, the food, and the many weirdnesses of this new world. Jacob's funny and perceptive observations will resonate, and readers will feel as if they've been there themselves. A terrific read for the 8-12 crowd.

—Margaret Meacham
Author of over 15 children's books including
The Ghosts of Laurelford, The Survival of Sarah Landing,
A Fairy's Guide to Living with Humans,
Oyster Moon, and *Secret of Heron Creek.*

This wonderful read brought back many happy memories of our four years living in Tokyo. Each day gave my family new and exciting memories to cherish. But I imagine that we also left the Japanese with many shocking memories of us and our American culture. One such memory was that of the gaijin (us) putting milk and sugar into our morning rice.

—Loralie Parks
Retired School Teacher

TRADING PIZZA FOR RAMEN

BRENDA LYNNE COHEN

ethos
collective

Published by Ethos Collective™
PO Box 43, Powell, OH 43065
Ethoscollective.vip

Identifiers:

LCCN: 2022911087

Paperback ISBN: 978-1-63680-079-0
Hardback ISBN: 978-1-63680-080-6
eBook ISBN: 978-1-63680-081-3

Available in paperback, hardback, and e-book

Dedicated to Mom, Dad, and Peter

Contents

CHAPTER ONE

The News

SOMETIMES AFTER SCHOOL, you have baseball practice or hang with a friend. Sometimes your parents drop a bomb on your lap, and your entire life explodes. This is how it all began, eating pizza with Mom.

It's Thursday after school, and the twins are at swim class. For one short hour, Mom and I can eat pizza at our favourite spot in peace while Dylan and Lily practise not drowning.

"Jacob, did you remember to wash your hands after baseball?" Mom asks.

"Yes." Sometimes she forgets that I'm thirteen and not six.

"Jacob?" she asks. It isn't a question. We both know I didn't wash my hands.

"Got it." I head to the bathroom. Seriously. My hands aren't that dirty.

I hold my hands up for Mom to see. "Clean. Can I eat now?" I ask.

She nods and smiles.

"There's a pizza tossing competition next month downtown; can we go?" I ask.

"We'll have to see. I think your dad may have something planned." She slowly starts sipping her tea.

That was vague. I know whenever Mom says, "We'll have to see," it always means no, but for some reason, she isn't willing to tell me.

"But I didn't even tell you what day it is."

"We'll have to see." She drinks more tea.

The hour of peace is gone. Here comes double trouble, my twin siblings.

"OK, load up. We're heading home. Dad has some news," Mom says as she directs us towards the van. She hastily throws the wet towels into the trunk and slams it shut. She is mumbling something to herself, but I can't make it out.

"What news?" I ask again.

"You'll see," she says. Just another "we'll have to see." I'm getting nowhere with this.

I eat my last slice of pizza in front of the television. I keep one eye on the screen and the other on Mom fidgeting in the kitchen. The twins are busy digging in the dirt in the backyard because that's what fourth-graders do after school. It is eerily quiet in the house as we wait for Dad to come home.

"Hey, team. I'm home," Dad calls from the back door. He likes to refer to us as his "team." No one answers.

"Dad!" Dylan yells as he marches in the door, "Lily is waving a giant beetle in my face!"

"Lily! Stop it!" Dad yells out at the patio door.

"Dad!" I say, trying to get his attention.

"Lily!" he calls again.

"Dad!" I yell at him. He turns to Mom and me.

"The kids want to hear your news," Mom says in a sing-song voice.

"Oh, you didn't tell them?" Dad seems surprised.

She gives him a look. "Uh, no."

I press on. "Your news? What is your news?" Seriously, what's a kid got to do to get an answer around here? Lily and Dylan stop fighting long enough to listen. Mom and Dad look at each other, they look at me, look at each other again, and say in unison: "WE'RE MOVING TO JAPAN!"

"In four weeks," says Dad cautiously, looking at Mom. She drops a frying pan on the floor. I suspect she was aiming for his foot.

CHAPTER TWO

Packing and Letters

"MOM! MOM!" LILY'S screaming again. It's been two weeks since the announcement, and our house smells like cardboard and packing tape. Have you seen the movie *Home Alone*? Me neither. Apparently, there is this family that goes on vacation and forgets one of the kids at home. I'm wondering if one of us will get left behind in the chaos of this move.

I've been hiding things under my bed so Mom doesn't decide to pack them in a box marked "storage." I'm not sure where the "storage" boxes are going, but I know it's not Tokyo.

Yesterday, Mom asked me to help Dylan and Lily write letters to their clubs, telling them we are moving. Lily's went something like this:

Dear Redmond Reptile Rescue,

I am sorry, but I will no longer be able to volunteer at the rescue centre on Monday and Wednesday after school. We are moving to Japan. My dad says I can still be a member if I pay my dues. I hope that you will take yen as payment.

Please remind Peter that Felix, the two-headed red-eared slider turtle, does not like the heat lamp on the south side of his tank. I don't know why he keeps moving it there. He likes it on the north side, where it shines closer to his floating dock.

On Mondays, I feed the hissing cockroaches for Suzanne. Please make sure she knows to feed them that day. Also, they like squash or pumpkin best. Stop feeding them carrots.

From,
Lily E. Cooper

You have to admire her nerve in telling the owner, Peter, how to take care of his turtles. I am sure the rescue centre will live on without her. Still, chances are they will never find another nine-year-old who knows the difference between a sulcata tortoise and any other kind of tortoise. Or someone who can spell tortoise, for that matter. Lily also had to return the various pets she was housing for them, a cockroach named Sugar and a bright orange milk snake named Sunny. I will miss Sunny only because she terrifies Dylan.

Dylan's letter was a little easier to manage:

Jeff,

I am moving to Japan. I won't be attending Friday game night anymore. Sorry. You better make sure Cameron doesn't become the new Rocket League champion while I am gone.

See you online,
Dylan

I refused to write a letter to my baseball team. The team already knows that Dad's making us move three weeks before the big tournament. There is nothing left to say. They already replaced my position at second base with Chester. There is no way that guy can anticipate plays the way I do. Chester can hit, but he's terrible at defence. Who puts a heavy hitter who's slow on his feet at second base? Good luck with the double plays, Chester. Have fun muddying my position, Chester. Dufus.

"Mom!!!" yells Lily again.

"Yes, Lily, what is it?" asks Mom in her tired, not-right-now voice.

"I just read that Japanese people eat whales. Whales, Mom. Whales." Lily is holding her tablet and wildly pointing at a news article.

"And . . . ?" asks Mom.

"Well, I am not eating whale. Ever," Lily declares and storms away.

"So much for Whale Flipper Fridays," I half-heartedly joke to Mom. She tiredly smiles and gives me a gentle pat on the back before adding another roll of tape to her tape gun.

We are packing like mad so we can have the whole summer, almost four months, in Tokyo before school starts. Dad says it will help us settle in and get used to the city. All this packing has made Mom's hair wide and tall, frizzy and stringy, like a giant bird's nest on top of her head. I swear I saw some twigs in there yesterday. If someone doesn't tell her soon, a squirrel might move in, and I'm pretty sure they won't let you on an airplane with a live animal nesting in your hair.

"Jacob," Dad calls from the front door.

"Why are you home?" I ask. It's four on a Wednesday.

"Can't a dad come home early to hang out with his kids?" he says.

"I guess so," I respond. Not that Dad ever does.

"I need to drop something off at the Conners' house. Feel like a walk?" he asks.

"Sure."

Dad is carrying a box full of yard tools. He is busy explaining that we don't need yard tools in Tokyo because we won't have a yard. *Blah, blah, blah.* Wait—we won't have a yard?

"What do you mean we won't have a yard?" I ask.

"We are moving into an apartment building. It doesn't have a backyard," Dad explains.

"But where am I going to practise?" I ask.

"I'm sure we can find a park close by."

"I hate Tokyo already."

"Jacob, it's different. Sometimes 'different' can be exciting."

"But there is no yard, no baseball team, and none of my friends. I bet they don't even have pizza."

"You'll make friends and find a new baseball team."

"I don't want a new baseball team. I want my team."

"I know, Jacob." Dad stops and puts the box down. He gives me a bone-crushing hug. I don't want a hug. I want my life back.

7

"Nothing is ever going to be the same," I say as I pull away.

"Remember when you hated pizza, then tried it and became pizza obsessed? You won't know if you like Tokyo until you give it a try," he says as he picks up the box.

"Tokyo isn't pizza," I say.

"But it's not the end of the world either."

So he says.

We drop the box at the Conners' and make our way back home in silence. As we walk into the house, Dylan calls from the den. "Jacob, you've got to come and see this!"

He's been online researching obscure Japanese video games and our new neighbourhood most of the day.

"I found a pizza place for you," Dylan says. He shifts away from the laptop and shows me the website for a Pizza Hut in Tokyo.

"Pizza Hut isn't bad," I tell him. Finally, something that will stay the same.

"Check out today's specials. Bacon makes everything better," Dylan says as he laughs and flops on the couch. I scroll down the page, and there it is: "Today's special, a tasty blend of popcorn shrimp, mayo, ketchup, corn, seaweed strips, and bacon."

Now it's my turn to scream. "Mom! Mom!"

CHAPTER THREE

Departures

FOUR WEEKS. FORTY paper cuts. Four hundred boxes. Now we are waiting for our flight to Japan. Over the last month, I've been annoyed about the move, but now, as we stand in the security line, I am thinking this may be an opportunity.

Most of these people at the airport are leaving for a vacation. After a week or so, they will head home to the same old routine. I'm about to become an expat—I learned that's short for *expatriate*—like a rebel, an outlander. A person who lives in different places. A person with experience and knowledge of the world. I'm going to return home a kid who knows things that my friends will never get the chance to learn.

If my parents are forcing this to happen, taking me from my team and home, then I'm going to spring train the hell out of this. No one will even recognize me. I'll ramble off in foreign languages and slam hard to hit pitches only Japanese players know. I'm going to return as an All-Star Expat.

But first, let's discuss this lukewarm airport pizza. I can't believe this is the last slice I will have on home turf.

"Mom, this pizza is an abomination. An insult to the American dream," I declare.

"Just eat it, Jacob. I don't know what kind of food they'll have on the plane." Mom says as she shifts her weight to manage all the bags she is carrying. One is full of plane snacks, and the other two have all the important stuff she doesn't trust anyone to touch.

The security line is taking longer than usual. Lily's bag goes through the scanner and gets sent to the "additional check" area. Mom looks surprised. Lily takes security measures very seriously and typically has everything packed perfectly with little labelled Ziploc bags.

"Additional check" never happens to Lily. Dad, sure. I mean, he's got enough electronics in his carry-on to build an airplane navigation system while onboard. But Lily? Never.

"It must be a mistake, Mom," she says while we head over for the additional inspection.

"I'm sure you forgot some water in your bag or something, Lily; it's fine."

"Mom, I triple-checked. You know I triple-checked."

"It's fine, Lily." Mom reassures her. The security agent opens Lily's bag, and safely secured in a labelled Ziploc bag is Sugar, the cockroach.

"Lily!" screams Mom.

"Wow!" says the security guard as he takes a giant step backward.

"You promised to take that thing back to the rescue centre," Mom says.

"But I just couldn't leave Sugar behind. She's my favourite pet," Lily begs.

"Pet?" says the security agent. Lily thinks this is an invitation.

"Yes, her name is Sugar. She's a Madagascar hissing cockroach." She pulls the Ziploc bag out of her suitcase and holds it up to the man.

"Hissss," says Sugar.

Lily continues, "I knew she would be fine on the trip. I mean, cockroaches can live without water for a week."

Now I'm pretty sure this security guy has seen just about everything, but I doubt he woke up this morning expecting to see a little girl with a hissing cockroach in her carry-on. He turns to Mom. "That's not going on the plane."

"Of course not," Mom says apologetically and takes the bag from Lily.

"What?!" Lily cries and reaches for the bag. The two of them start arguing.

"Give it to me," Mom says.

"No!" Lily yells.

"Give it to me, Lily!"

"No!"

"Hiss!" Sugar screams.

You think you've seen pandemonium at security before? Wait until a mammoth-sized Madagascar hissing cockroach gets ripped from her plastic bag prison and flung across the room towards a crowd of unsuspecting passengers.

"Get it!" yells Mom.

"EEEEE!!!" screams some woman. Dylan attempts to reassure her that it's just a "stupid bug," but she's having none of it.

"Sugar, Sugar, come here, honey," calls Lily.

Bodies are pushing and shoving. Security guards are blocking the exits. Some man is stabbing at what he thinks is Sugar with his walking stick. Babies are crying. Businessmen are complaining about the wait. Backup security is running towards us. One guard has his hand on his gun. Things. Are. Out. Of. Control.

"Got it!" yells some man. Everyone stops to look. Lily's eyes are full of hope. He lifts his shoe, and there is pulverized Sugar. Let's call it Powdered Sugar.

The security guard zips up Lily's bag and hands it off to Mom. "Have a safe flight," he says.

"Thank you, sir," Mom says. "Lily, thank the man." Lily looks at Mom in disbelief; a large round snot bubble is forming around her nose. Tears are all over her face. Mom tightens her lips and widens her eyes at Lily.

"Thank (sniff) you (sniff)," Lily cries.

We manage to arrive at the gate without any more security breaches.

"Jacob, can you move your bag so I can sit down?" Dad asks. He has returned from the coffee shop with drinks. "Enjoy this cup," he tells Mom. "The coffee on the airplane is made of toilet water." Dad says stuff like that.

They call for boarding, and we find our seats. "Did you put on your seatbelt?" Mom nags. I told you that she forgets I'm thirteen, right?

Lily pulls out her notebook. She is still crying. I wonder if she's writing a goodbye letter to her cockroach in that notebook.

Lily has been telling strangers for weeks that we are moving to Japan and has the opinions of nearly twenty people on the topic. She is putting them in a small, glittery notebook with a turtle on the front. Dad said she should start a blog, but Lily is more interested in which gel pen colour matches the information she is adding to each page:

Tokyo is expensive (green pen).
The trains are crowded (purple pen).
They have cool gadgets (black pen).
They love comic books (pink pen).
The summers are hot (orange pen).

My favourite advice came from this guy at the mall who warned us, "Don't drink anything that sounds like the word cow piss" (yellow pen). Cow piss? Who would drink cow piss?

I watch Dad follow his airplane routine. It's the same thing every time we fly. He puts his bag in the overhead compartment, then removes, folds, and secures his coat on top of it. He then proceeds to take off his shoes and neatly put them under his seat. To finish, he puts on his noise-cancelling headphones and blocks out everything around him, including us. He will sit like this until the food cart arrives, and he orders a tomato juice. He read somewhere that tomato juice tastes better at 30,000 feet.

Mom is reading a Japan travel guide. You can see the pages she has folded over and highlighted. She has gone from being super stressed about packing to hyper-planning mode. At least the squirrel nest is gone, or it's in one of those bags she crammed into the overhead compartment, and it will jump out and attack someone once we land.

Dylan has a Japanese manga (comic book) on his lap, and he's busy rifling through his snacks. He'll have them all eaten or all on the floor before take-off. Never share popcorn with him at the movies. I wonder if they have an English movie theatre in Japan.

I close my eyes and try to picture the fog resting on the outfield just before Sunday practice. The crack of the bat as I hit a long ball past second base. The taste of the dirt kicking up as I start to run. The call of my friends cheering me on. Coach yelling, "Faster, faster!" I begin to drift off.

"Jacob, what colour says 'origami' to you?" shrieks Lily.

CHAPTER FOUR

Arrivals

AS THE PLANE starts to descend into Narita International Airport, I look out the window and see lights and buildings for miles. I'm going to get lost in this place. Not lost the way Lily gets lost when she heads into the woods but lost like I might forget who I am in a place so big. I take a moment to think about home. Redmond may be on the outskirts of Seattle, but Seattle itself is a decent-sized town. We have an NFL team, MLB team, MLS team, rush-hour traffic, skyscrapers, buses, streetcars, trains—deep breath. I can do this. All-Star Expat.

The plane lands. The seat belt light goes off.

"Jacob. Take a bag." Mom is throwing a suitcase at me while she attempts to clean the garbage and crumbs from Dylan's seat. "Honestly, Dylan, would it kill you to clean up for once?!"

Dylan is standing and sleeping at the same time while Lily is still drooling on her window. No one dares to wake her until the line starts moving.

"We're here! Who's excited?!" It's Dad. He slept. Maybe next time we fly, I'll try the noise-cancelling headphones and tomato juice.

We split into two taxis with our ten suitcases. Dad and I sneak into the first one and leave Mom with the cranky twins. Inside, the seats are white cloth, and the driver wears white gloves. The doors open and close automatically. The taxi is spotless. I look behind to check on the others and see Lily already asleep, leaning on the car window. That's going to leave a stain.

The highway and skyscrapers go on forever.

"Amazing, isn't it?" Dad says as the taxi switches to yet another major highway.

"How many people live here?" I ask him.

"About 35 million," Dad says.

"In Japan?" I ask.

"In Tokyo," he replies.

"Geez. I think a few million are on the roads tonight," I say. Dad laughs casually and puts his arm around my neck.

"You're going to love it," he tells me.

When we arrive at the hotel, there is a policeman out front and a construction crew washing graffiti off a bench.

"Looks like there was vandalism or something," Dad says. "The Japanese take property crime very seriously, so don't go breaking anything or drawing on walls."

"Sure, Dad," I respond. Seriously, it was that one time, and who visits the back of the library anyhow?

Two of Dad's Japanese coworkers are waiting for us inside the lobby. One of them repeatedly bows as he introduces himself and apologizes for the distraction outside. The other coworker gives us a bunch of wrapped gifts. She nods and smiles a lot. She heads to the front desk to get our room keys, and the hotel staff sing *Konbanwa* in unison.

The lady comes back with our keys and tells us *Konbanwa* means "good evening." Mom attempts to repeat it and says something like "cabana."

There are warm face cloths in the hallway to clean our hands, and there are slippers just inside the hotel room for our feet. They come with instructions to remove our shoes and leave them by the door. I am starting to think the Japanese have a minor obsession with cleanliness. How on earth is Dylan going to survive here?

As soon as we have all the bags in the room, Lily tears into one of the gift packages. It is a box of apples, each one wrapped in plastic and sealed with a very official-looking sticker.

"Don't touch them!" Mom yells at Lily. "They're a gift."

"Yeah, for us," Lily says back.

"Leave them, Lily!" she warns. I think Mom is afraid to eat something wrapped up so nicely. I longingly look at the apples until I fall asleep.

● ● ●

I open my eyes. It's dark—dumb jetlag. The twins and Dad are snoring. Dad's snore is conflicting with the tempo of the twins. He is breathing in while they breathe out. I hate the duelling snores. I'm starving. I hate this stuffy hotel room. I'm hungry. I hate sharing a bed with the twins. I want a pizza.

I look at the clock: 5:00 a.m. I unwrap one of the apples with ninja stealth. Stop. Check on Mom. She's sleeping. I slowly bite into it. The apple is delicious.

Shuffling out from under the covers, I peek out the window of our hotel room. We are forty stories up, and I can still hear the hum of the city. Every muscle in my body is tight, and my right eye won't stop twitching. The hotel room smells like stale airplane air, leather luggage, and sleep farts. Below, I see the flashing array of signs and streetlights and hear the buzzing motorcycles, taxis, and people.

"Jacob. Did you eat one of the apples?" Mom is up.

"Yes." There is no point in lying; the evidence is there. She rubs her eyes, climbs out of bed, and comes to sit next to me at the window.

"Was it tasty?" she asks.

"Not bad," I reply. Mom reaches for one and unwraps it as she takes her first bite and puts her arm around me.

"You OK?" she asks.

"Just can't sleep."

"Jetlag?"

"Yeah, jetlag."

"Do you want to go for a walk?" she asks.

"Sure."

I pull on some pants and search for my shoes in the darkness. Oh, right, the front door. I wonder about Japanese kids. Do they wipe off with a warm towel as they remove their shoes at the front door when they come home? Do they get individually wrapped apples in their lunch boxes? Do they have a white cloth covering their car seats?

Mom interrupts my train of thought and whispers, "OK, let's go." As we sneak out the door, we leave a note on the side table for the snoring choir: Gone for food.

The lobby is quiet. The staff greets us with a big smile, a small bow, and a unified *ohayo gozaimasu*. I'm guessing that means good morning.

As we exit the hotel, the warm, sticky summer heat hits us. Mom stops in her tracks as if she is considering turning back into the air-conditioned lobby.

"C'mon," I tell her. "I'm starving."

"Right. Right," Mom says in a daze. The jetlag, the heat. I get it.

The crowds are less chaotic than they appeared from the hotel window. It's crowded, but somehow, people are almost skating around one another. A friend of mine who travelled to Asia told me that everyone pushes and shoves. This morning in Tokyo—with the sweltering heat, rushing crowds, and tiny sidewalks—somehow, there is no pushing. It's as if each person has unique echolocation senses like a bat. They move silently around one another, and if two strangers graze arms, they stop and say something.

Mom and I haven't honed our echolocation skills yet. We are bumping elbows with everyone. I start to listen to the words they say each time we hit.

"Sami." No, that's not it.

Bump. "Sumi something." Almost there.

Crash! "*Sumima* something."

Bump! "*Sumimasen.*" That's it.

Bump! "*Sumimasen.*"

Bump! "*Sumimasen!*" I got it. The "sorry-I-got-into-your-personal-space-and-knocked-you" word. "*Sumimasen.*"

"What will you have?" Mom asks me as we stand in front of a Starbucks just as they unlock the door. Really? We come to Japan, and our first meal is at Starbucks? At least I know what I want.

"I'll have two chocolate croissants, a banana, vanilla steamed milk, and an apple juice."

The girl behind the cash register looks nervous that we are her first customers. Mom makes it easy for the cashier as she points at the menu and then at the food in the display case. As Mom puts money on the counter, the cashier seems panicked and is shifting her look from Mom to me to the barista on her left. Why is she nervous? Something is wrong. Then I see it.

"Mom, can't you use an app or a credit card or something?" I ask.

"Why, is that not enough?" Mom asks.

"No, Mom, look—you gave her an airline ticket." I point down to the crumbled ticket she placed on the counter.

"Oh, shoot. Sorry," Mom says. She reaches back into her pocket. Mom starts rambling. She tells the cashier that we have jet lag and barely slept, that her husband is snoring away while we all starve in a tiny hotel room. That all she has eaten is a perfectly wrapped red apple that was "surprisingly delightful." The cashier looks like she is going to pass out from the embarrassment.

"Mom, she doesn't speak English," I remind her. Mom ignores me and keeps talking. I reach for the only Japanese word I know.

"*Sumimasen*," I say quickly.

The cashier bows her head and replies, "*Sumimasen*."

Mom raises her eyebrows at me, pays with the tap of her phone, and we leave with our breakfast.

"Wow. Well done, Jacob; when did you learn that word?" Mom asks.

"Ten minutes ago," I say through a mouthful of croissant.

"You're going to be just fine here," she says as she rubs the top of my head. She does this when she is proud of me. I pull away.

Bump! "Ah, *Sumimasen*," I apologize to a stranger.

CHAPTER FIVE

The Park

"WELCOME HOME!" DAD says as he opens the main door to the apartment building.

"Where's the backyard?" Lily asks.

"There is a playground down the street," Dad replies. Lily snorts her nose and rolls her eyes a little.

"And which place is ours?" asks Dylan.

"201," Dad says as he leads us around the corner of the main lobby and to the stairs. "We just go up one flight of stairs and *voilà!*" Dad is pointing at a giant metal door with 201 written on it. We're crammed into the dimly lit stairwell, it's a thousand degrees, and our bags and bodies are pushing against one another.

"Why is the door made of metal?" Lily asks.

"Earthquakes," Dad answers.

"Earthquakes?!" Lily yells. Her voice echoes in the tiny stairwell.

"Hush," Mom scolds Dad.

"What?" Dad asks.

Dylan chimes in, "What do you mean earthquakes?"

"Japan has lots of earthquakes, guys. Didn't anyone read the information packet I gave you on our new home?" Dad is trying to get the door unlocked, but he's taking forever. He keeps turning the key right, taking it out, turning it left, taking it out, turning it upside down, left, right side up, left.

"This isn't my home!" Lily screams and starts to sniffle. Mom comforts her while holding two suitcases and trying not to fall down the stairs.

"OK, earthquakes, but why the metal door?" Dylan keeps on.

"What's the holdup?" Mom barks.

"I'm working on it. It won't open." Dad is starting to lose his cool.

"Why the metal door?" Dylan asks.

"I refuse to live somewhere without a backyard," Lily declares.

"The door?" Mom prods.

"Working on it," Dad says.

"I hate Japan. I hate Japan," Lily mutters.

"But what does a metal door have to do with an earthquake?" Dylan wants to know.

"Fires, Dylan, earthquakes and fires!" Dad huffs.

"FIRE?!" Lily squeaks.

"Door!!" Mom snaps.

You know when you're cooking pizza, and you have that few seconds between a perfectly crispy crust with bubbling cheese and a burnt mess? We're about ten seconds from a burnt mess. I push past Mom and blubbering Lily; I squeeze past Dylan, who is still looking at the metal door with a stupid

22

look on his face, and hand my bag to Dad. I grab the key, push it into the lock, turn left, and open the door.

"There," I remove the key and give it back to Dad.

"Thanks," Dad says, "welcome home."

There's whining and screaming behind us. "Sounds like home," I reply as I push my way into the apartment.

I quickly scan the living area. There is some ugly rental furniture and one large, long, rectangular cardboard box suspiciously placed in the middle of the room.

"What do you think it is?" Dylan asks me from behind.

"I don't know."

"A dead body?" he asks.

"Maybe."

"A dead body? What are you talking about?" It's Lily.

"That." I point to the box.

The three of us pause and slowly walk toward the box. Dylan stands at one end and smells the corner. He moves to the other end and gives it a quick sniff. He shrugs his shoulders. Lily leans in a little closer to examine any markings. She scans the sides and the top for any stamps, addresses, or labels. Nothing. I carefully place my finger on the top flap and pull it back.

"What is it?" Lily's standing farther back now and is trying to peek over my shoulder.

Just then, Mom chimes in, "Oh, you found the box. The people who moved out said they left a few toys."

Lily pushes through and pulls open the box. Sure enough, it's a bunch of toys. She's busy sifting through a bag of dolls and rolling her eyes. "Ugh. Girl toys." I'm sure if she keeps looking, she'll find a bug or beetle.

"Hey, check this out. It's a unicycle." Dylan pulls the one-wheel bike out of the box. He tries to get on it. Falls. He tries again. Falls. I grab the unicycle from him and give it a go. I crash into the coffin-like box, and toys come pouring out.

"Mom!" yells Lily. Suddenly, she cares about all the girl toys.

"What?" Mom yells from the kitchen.

"Dylan and Jacob are riding a bike in the living room!" she yells.

"It's a unicycle!" Dylan corrects her.

"What?" Mom calls back.

"Dylan and Jacob are riding a uni-bike in the living room!" she yells louder.

"A what?" Mom says as she walks into the living room. "Boys, you're going to have to take that outside."

"There's no backyard," Dylan protests.

"There's a park a block away. Just left out the front door," Dad pipes in.

"We're going to the park!" I yell, and the two of us fly out the front door before Mom says no.

It is hot and sticky outside. Luckily, it only takes a minute to find the park—well, a patch of grass and swings.

Dylan tosses me the unicycle. "This thing is impossible!"

"Don't be a Chester. Watch and learn," I tell him as the older, more experienced brother. I sit on the seat and get one foot off the ground and crash. Yeah, it's impossible.

"Maybe if we lean it up against the water fountain, we can get on easier." Dylan has a plan. I rest my foot on the lower tap and lean the bike on the fountain to balance. "One. Twoooo. Three," I count before falling into the mud.

"Awesome!" Dylan grabs the bike to try.

"*Sugoi!*" yells a voice from the swings. We look over to see a Japanese boy about my age. His hair covers his eyes like he wants to be the lead singer of a boy band, and he's wearing a San Francisco Giants T-shirt, but the logo is wrong.

"When did that kid get here?" I ask Dylan.

"Don't know."

"Hey," I call over to him.

"Hi," he says back as he walks toward us.

"You visiting Tokyo?" he asks. His English seems pretty good.

"No. We just moved here."

"Ah . . . so. You go to school?"

"Not yet; we start after summer. Hey, what's up with your Giants shirt?"

"You like Yomiuri Giants?" He is all excited.

"Who?"

"Yomiuri Giants!" he points at his shirt.

"No, San Francisco Giants," I correct him, and now he looks a little annoyed.

"No, Yomiuri Giants," he insists.

He points to the unicycle. "*Sugoi-ne!*" he says.

I give him another blank look. "Unicycle," I correct him.

"*Sugoi!*" he says.

"No, unicycle," I repeat.

"*Sugoi* means awesome; your uni-bicycle is awesome," he says in English.

"Thanks; want to try?" I offer the unicycle to him. He takes it from me and nods politely. He continues to nod as he pushes past Dylan and leans the bike against the water fountain. He lifts one leg to get on the bike and falls face-first into the mud. Dylan bursts into laughter and yells, "*Sugoi!*" I give him a quick punch to the arm. He snorts and tries to hold it in.

The kid stands up, shakes off the mud, and looks at me with a bright red face. I turn over my hands, showing him the dirt from my fall. Our eyes meet. He starts to laugh—a slow, quiet laugh. One that makes you wonder if he's going to secretly fill your shoes with snakes when you turn your head.

"Do you want to try again?" Dylan asks.

"OK," he says. He takes the unicycle and tries again. We all continue to take turns, but I keep a close eye on him. There's something different about this kid. I think he's having fun, but he's stiff and serious.

On my turn, I get the unicycle away from the fountain and am peddling in a circle for at least five seconds when it happens. I feel a small, wet, muddy hand push me over. My left foot gets stuck in the peddle; I wave my arms around for balance, and my right foot goes flying around, searching for something to hold.

"Watch out!" I hear Dylan scream as I slam into the water fountain, and my foot pushes down on the lower faucet, breaking the tap from the foundation and sending a geyser of water rushing into the air.

"He pushed me," I shouted at Dylan, but it was too late. The kid's already running away. The two of us are standing in the waterfall.

"Turn it off," I scream at Dylan.

"It's broken."

"What do you mean it's broken?"

"You stepped on it and broke it."

"Broke what?"

"The tap."

"The tap?"

Dylan fiddles with the tap. It's no use. He pulls on the unicycle. No use.

"Mom's gonna kill us," I say.

"Let's get outta here."

"What about the unicycle?"

"What *about* the unicycle?"

"It's stuck on the broken tap." I look down. The unicycle is stuck on the broken tap and making a giant lake of the playground.

"Leave it," I tell Dylan.

"Leave it?"

"Leave it."

"What do we tell Mom?" he asks as we start running for home.

"I don't understand. You gave the unicycle to a little girl?" Mom asks for the third time.

"We let her try it out, and she was so good that we thought she should have it," I lie.

"You gave it to a little girl?" Mom asks again, putting a Band-Aid on Dylan's arm and staring intensely into his eyes and straight to his very soul.

"Yes. Yes. Just like Jacob said," he lies.

"You gave it to a little girl," Mom says.

"Yes, a little girl," I lie. "Can we go check out our rooms now?" I start to back away, pushing Dylan with me. Mom stands still and watches us suspiciously. "OK," she says and goes back to making lunch.

"Holy crap, that was close," I say to Dylan as we lock ourselves in our empty bedroom.

"I don't think she bought it," he says.

"Doesn't matter as long as Dad doesn't know that we damaged public property. But that kid worries me. He may rat on us."

"What kid?" Dylan asks.

"Sly."

"Who?"

"That kid at the park with the weird Giants T-shirt."

"He seemed alright to me."

"Dylan, you have a lot to learn."

CHAPTER SIX

Ramen

TWO DAYS LATER, Dad stops us at breakfast. "Did you guys find the playground around the corner?" he asks.

"No," we reply in unison.

"Looks like there was vandalism or something," Dad says. "Remember, the Japanese take property crime very seriously," he adds.

"I know, Dad," I reply.

"OK," he says and taps me on the back. It feels like a gentle warning.

"Tonight, I thought it would be fun if we all went out for ramen. Try out some traditional food," he says.

I've been looking forward to trying traditional ramen since Japanese pizza and hamburgers are disgusting. Sure, the Pizza Hut and Dominos varieties are pretty standard, but everywhere else is a mess of garlic bread meets ketchup meets sprinkling of some random white cheeses.

"Oh, that sounds lovely!" Mom is overly enthusiastic. She does this when she's trying to get us on board with one of Dad's ideas.

"Sure."

"Whatever."

"Do they serve whale?"

"No, Lily, they do not serve whale."

"OK, then."

● ● ●

The ramen restaurant is easy to find. It's a tiny doorway with a giant steamy bowl of noodles floating above it. As we walk through the door, a curtain in the doorway sweeps over our faces and shoulders, and we are greeted with the customary cry of "*Irasshaimase!*" from the staff. I've discovered this means "welcome." You hear it every time you enter a store, restaurant, or building. Some places have an automatic system where a robot chimes in, "*Irasshaimase!*" It's like Alexa or Siri welcoming you home every time you enter. Creepy.

The owners of the ramen place look like they've been welcoming guests for a LONG time. They both have hunched backs and few teeth and wear traditional Japanese robes and slippers. The restaurant is tiny, with one side of the house set up with tables and chairs and the other with traditional Japanese seating—low tables on the floor and cushions to sit on. The lady smiles, bows, and leads us to a table.

"Oh, Yoshioka san, can we please sit over there?" Dad points to the low tables and floor seating.

"*Hi, hi,*" the lady says and leads us to the tables on the floor. I think Dad is trying too hard to give us the complete experience. I just want to eat.

As I try to find a way to comfortably sit on the floor with nothing to lean my back against, I notice Dad has crossed his legs into some yoga pose.

"This is the most comfortable way to sit," he tells me. Now I know he's definitely trying too hard. Dylan has given up and is leaning against the wall about two feet from the table. He has wrapped his arms around his knees and is playing a game on his phone. Lily seems perfectly content to kneel and starts to play with all of the various little dishes. I stretch my legs under the table and lean back on my elbows.

"Jacob, you are kicking me," Mom complains.

"Just move over a little."

"Why don't you bring your legs back to your side?"

"And put them where?"

"I don't know."

"Mom?!"

"Fine. Fine." Mom moves over a little and lets me rest my feet next to her. I'm not sure how I'm going to eat like this.

The man arrives with our tea. I'm impressed by how he manages to get his tired, old body to squat down and sit on his knees and pour each of us a cup. He smiles at Dad and bows.

"Yoshioka san and his wife have had this restaurant for forty years." Dad goes on, "Their ramen is the best. You're going to love it." Dad goes ahead and orders for all of us.

The first course is a salad served in a tiny little dish. The dressing is good, but I don't get why it needs to have corn on top. Then there is another small dish with something pickled, with corn on the side, followed by a cup of piping hot miso soup with, you guessed it, corn floating in it. My legs are cramping, and my back is killing me.

"Where's the ramen?" I ask.

You can see the steam coming from the kitchen as Yoshioka san and his wife carry the trays with our ramen. I quickly look in my bowl. Yes! They must have run out of corn.

My steaming bowl of soup broth has chunks of pork, seaweed, lots of garlic, green onion, some strange-looking flower-shaped white and pink ERASER, and a couple of boiled eggs. It's kind of like the soup version of an "everything-but-the-kitchen-sink" pizza.

I'm not a picky eater, but I swear there is an eraser in my soup. "Dad, why is there an eraser in my soup?"

"It's called Naruto. It's fish. Just eat it; it's delicious."

"Dylan, stop picking stuff out!" Mom is heckling Dylan from the other side of the table, but we all know it's no use. Dylan is the pickiest eater I know. By the time he is done dissecting his soup, there'll be nothing but broth and pork. There is no point in stopping him, or he'll starve.

I dive my spoon into the bowl and shove pieces of food onto it with my chopsticks. It's salty. Sweet. Bacon-y. Soft. Crunchy. Hot! Hot! My nose is running, and my mouth is burning, but honestly, this may be my new favourite food. I could put anything in this soup. It's like crafting your pizza from scratch. However, that fish-flavoured eraser has got to go. I carefully pick it out of my soup and pass it to Dad with my chopsticks.

Suddenly, there is a scream. An ear-piercing, toe-curling cry and a swift, wrinkly hand comes out of nowhere and slaps my chopsticks down to the table. The fish eraser flies across the room and lands on the floor. Dad is motionless and stunned. Mrs. Yoshioka is standing in front of us with a frown on her face and her karate chop hand still in midair.

"What the . . ." Dylan starts to say as Mom kicks him under the table.

A familiar voice comes from behind me, "It is rude to pass food with your chopsticks. In Japan, we do that with bones at funerals. Not at dinner time. You have upset my grandma." It's Sly. He's back—and at a convenient time, it seems.

"Hey, it's the kid from the park," Dylan says.

"What park?" Dad asks.

"The park," Dylan says.

"The park that was vandalized?" Dad asks.

"Yeah. What? No," Dylan says.

"Haru," Sly says to me. Our eyes lock.

"What?" I reply.

"Haru. My name is Haru."

"Oh." Am I supposed to introduce myself? Seriously, the kid pushed me over and ran away. Who does something like that? Everyone at the table is still and waiting for me to respond.

"Jacob," says Mom. "His name is Jacob."

"Thanks, Mom. I got this."

"Jacob, you're acting rude," she starts.

"Mom, you don't understand, when we were at the park with the unicycle—"

"And we gave it to the little girl," Dylan interrupts me.

"Oh. We—we met Sly, I mean Haru, on the way home," I conclude.

Haru is watching Dylan and me struggle with our lie. He is looking at each member of the family closely. He picks up my chopsticks from the table and hands me a new pair from the cabinet behind him. He slightly bows as he gives the new chopsticks to me. Moment of truth. Is he going to rat us out?

He speaks, "I am sorry for my *obaasan*. My grandma. She is very strict with table manners."

"And quick with her karate hands too," Dylan says. There is another awkward pause, and finally, everyone laughs.

Mrs. Yoshioka comes back to fill our teacups. "*Sumimasen*," I say to her. She bows slightly and reaches forward to fill my cup. I make sure to lean back and give her lots of room.

I walked home that night with a full stomach and mind. Sly—I mean Haru—kept our secret safe, but why did he push me at the park and take off? It just doesn't make sense.

We come to a busy crossing, and I look up to see a shiny advertisement; it's a baseball pitcher in mid-throw with fire shooting out behind him. He is wearing the same Giants shirt Haru was wearing. I quicken my pace to catch up with Dad. "Dad, Dad."

"Yeah, Jacob."

"Tell me again about the Japanese baseball league."

"What do you want to know? Baseball is huge in Japan. I swear you kids didn't read any of the stuff I gave you."

"Whatever. So baseball's big?"

"Really big."

"Is there a team called the Yom Giants?"

"Yes, the Yomiuri Giants or Tokyo Giants. We should go to a game sometime."

So I insulted Haru's baseball team. Is that why he acted all serious and pushed me in the mud? It seems like overkill to me.

CHAPTER SEVEN

The Baseball Diamond

WEEK TWO IN Tokyo. My jetlag is finally under control, and the rest of our stuff should arrive this week. Dylan, Lily, and I are out exploring and eating some tasty buns Lily brought along.

"These cheese buns are amazing," I tell Dylan as I shove another into my mouth. "This does not taste like Japanese food."

"That's because it's not," says Lily as she skips beside us. "We got them at the French bakery."

"French bakery? When did you find a French bakery?" I ask.

"Dad found one last night," says Dylan. Dad has been so busy with work; I haven't seen him since we went for ramen. When did he head to a French bakery? Dad is full of surprises, as is Tokyo.

"It's just around the corner," says Lily.

"The bakery?" I ask.

"No, the baseball diamond," she replies with a huge smile on her face. "Mom told me about it."

"Did you know about this?" I ask Dylan.

"Yeah. What else are we going to do? That ramen shop grandma's got her eye on us. We're not going that way." My fault. "The playground is flooded." Also my fault. "I know this weekend is the Redmond Baseball Tournament, and you're bummed about missing it." Dad's fault. "Come on, Jacob," he finishes.

"Come on, it'll be fun!" says Lily. Twins two. Jacob one. It's more of a dictatorship than a democracy when the twins band together.

"OK, OK. Let's find this baseball diamond," I say.

We turn the corner, and there is a regulation-size baseball field smack dab in the middle of our urban neighbourhood. It's crazy what they can squeeze into tiny places in this city. This morning, I saw a public toilet in the middle of the road built on the median no more than three feet wide and five feet long.

"Wow," says Dylan, "that is huge!"

Lily grabs the fence surrounding the field and stands on her tippy toes to see the other side. "It looks like a game is about to start!" she yells. A group of local girls sitting on the bleachers starts to giggle and laugh at her excitement. Japanese girls are always amazed at how loud Lily is. They also giggle a lot.

Four cheese buns later, I am thirsty. "Let's get a drink before we sit down," I say. We head over to the vending machines. There is one on every street corner. You can find candy, batteries, games, soup, magazines, you name it. Pretty much everything you need, you can buy in a vending machine in Tokyo.

"Look, Jacob," says Lily, once again a little too loudly. The girls giggle.

"Shh. Lily, what is it?" I ask.

"Look, that drink. It's called Calpis," she says.

"So what?" I ask.

"Calpis, Jacob. Calpis!" she says again. "What does that sound like to you?" I repeat the name a couple of times.

"It's the cow piss!" I yell. More giggles from the bleachers.

"What's going on here?" asks Dylan.

"A guy back home warned us about a drink that sounds like cow piss," I tell him. "This has to be it."

"We have to try it." Lily declares. She's already putting her change into the machine.

"Are you sure?" I ask her. The guy was clear with his advice: Stay away from cow piss.

"Oh, yeah. We're trying it." Lily pushes the button. The drink drops into the machine slot. We all quietly stare at it for a moment. Lily breaks the silence. "You first." She hands me the can.

"No way, it was your idea." I hand the can back to her.

"No, you do it!" she yells. After a few more passes, we reach the bleachers and sit down next to the girls.

"Whatever, I'll do it," says an irritated Dylan. He grabs the drink from Lily. He smiles and shrugs at the girl next to him. She covers her mouth and giggles.

"Here goes nothing," says Dylan. He takes a giant swig of cow piss. He pauses, looks at the girls on the bleachers, and says, "*Sugoi!*" They giggle. He passes the can to me.

"Here goes nothing," I say. I take a small sip. It tastes like a yogurt drink but thinner and bubbly, like soda. Imagine a can of cola mixed with rotten milk. It's terrible, but there is no way I am letting on until Lily tries it.

"Not bad," I say.

"Yeah, not bad," says Dylan.

I pass it to Lily. Her eyes are blinking very quickly as she looks at us. She's reading our faces and wondering if we are baiting her to drink it. Brothers do that.

She puts the can to her mouth and takes a sip. There's a pause. For a moment, I think that she might like it, but that passes quickly. "Pssst." She spits cow piss directly on the girls next to us.

Dylan and I break out into fits of laughter. Lily turns red. The girls aren't giggling now as they pack up their things and move to the other side of the bleachers. I think I heard them whisper, "*Gaijin*," a few times. I know that means "foreigner" or "outsider."

Dylan pulls himself together just long enough to ask, "Can I have it?" He takes the can from Lily and keeps drinking. The pickiest kid in the world is drinking cow piss. Japan is an alternate universe.

The baseball game is about to begin, so I move to a seat at the front. I want to see what Japanese baseball is all about.

The teams are warming up and stretching to classical music. It's like watching synchronized swimming in the field. No one is talking, joking, or laughing.

"Why are they so serious?" I say to no one in particular.

"The team that stretches as one in harmony, plays as one, and wins," says a voice behind me. I turn around to see a Japanese girl. She is sitting alone, drinking a can of coffee, and wearing a Yomiuri Giants hat with her hair tucked inside.

"You speak English?" I ask.

"Of course I speak English. I'm Yuki."

"Nice to meet you, Yuki. I'm Jacob."

"*Hajimemashite*," she responds. "Nice to meet you."

"Do you know these teams?" I ask.

"Yes. They're high school teams. My brother plays on the blue team." She points to an oddly tall guy stretching on the field. I think he's the pitcher.

"Why is everyone so serious?" I ask her.

"They aren't serious, just focusing. It's important to all be in unison. That's how we work better together," she explains.

"Is this a baseball thing?" I ask.

"No, it's a Japanese thing," Yuki says. She takes a large gulp of her coffee and shoots the empty can into the trash. "Score!" she calls out as she climbs over the bleacher to sit next to me. "See, in Japan, we don't care for hotshots. No player is better than the rest. Our teams work together, practise together, run together, and stretch together. No player is treated differently than the other," she says.

"There is always a player that's better than the rest," I argue. I am thinking about Chester and how he's probably letting a run go by as we speak.

"Maybe some players are better, but they aren't treated differently. In Japanese baseball, we play as one," she says. "You play baseball?" she asks.

"Yes. Well, not since we moved here. But back home, yes." I hate saying that.

"So you live in Tokyo?" she asks.

"We just moved here from Seattle. I'll be at the international school in September," I tell her as I point in what I think is the general direction of the school.

"That's where I go to school!" she says. "What grade?"

"Seven."

"Cool. I'll be in eight."

The players have finally finished stretching and are heading back to the dugout. I see a couple of them relax for a moment and laugh. Once they hit the benches, they are back to silence and waiting for instructions from their coach.

"Hey, how come you speak English so well?" I ask Yuki.

"I lived in Texas when I was little," she says.

"Was it weird moving from Tokyo to Texas?" I ask.

"Yeah," she replies. I finally found someone who understands how hard it is to move. Maybe she'll know how to stop missing home. Maybe she can help me figure out Tokyo. My mind is spinning. She has all the answers. What do I ask her?

"Can you ride a horse?" I blurt out. Honestly, it was the first thing to come to mind. She rolls her eyes at me.

"Are stereotypes your thing?" She mimics me, "Japanese are serious. Texans ride horses . . ."

"Find me a silly Japanese person and a Texan who can't ride a horse," I reply.

She raises her hands in the air and says, "Me!"

We watch a few innings, and suddenly, she starts packing up her stuff. "I have to go help my brother's team. I honestly don't think the coach has any idea what he's doing."

We exchange numbers, and she texts me a minute later—a horse emoji and a thumbs up. I give her a thumbs up from across the field. I think I've made my first Japanese friend.

CHAPTER EIGHT

The Shrine

MY HAND RUBS against the damp wall of the cave. I can touch both sides at the same time, and I think it's getting narrower as I venture deeper into the darkness. Why did I go first? Why did Dad drag us to another temple? Why is this one in a cave?

It's crazy dusty, and I can barely see in front of me. No, wait, that's not dust. It's smoke. Cough. It smells like perfume or wood chips or when Dad tries to barbeque something with fresh herbs. Gag. It must be burning incense. The Japanese love incense.

It's getting darker. I see there is light at the end of the cave, but I'm a little afraid of what else is in here. Bats live in caves and bears, scorpions, spiders, snakes—lots of things I don't want to meet in the dark. Dad told us about some wild snow monkeys that live in Japan. There better not be any of those in this cave.

Six weeks in Tokyo. Cue another family weekend adventure. This time, a two-hour train ride to Kamakura, a town south of Tokyo on the ocean. Dad promised us ice cream and beaches, but so far, we have seen a giant metal Buddha called Daibutsu and a hundred little shrines. Yes, the Buddha was forty feet tall, but other than its size, there wasn't much to see. We followed a hiking trail for almost an hour—which felt like two with Dylan at my heels—until we reached this cave-like shrine.

"Dad, are you sure this is the right place?" I call into the darkness.

"Yes, just keep moving; the temple is at the end," he calls from behind me.

Just as I get used to the darkness and the flowery smell, I hear something that concerns me. Rushing water. Fast, rushing water and falling metal.

"Dad, turn back. The cave is collapsing and filling with water!" I yell.

He reaches me and touches my shoulder from behind. "Calm down, Jacob. It's just the river where you wash your money."

Wash my money? Why would I wash money in a dark, creepy cave? What has Dad gotten us into this time?

Finally, I can see some light. There are hundreds of candles melting on the sides of the cave. The incense is burning in little metal dishes. It looks like something out of a horror movie where some old witch is going to show up and tear my face off and use my bones for stew. The others are catching up, and I can hear them from behind.

"Mom, look, I found a lovely cave spider," says Lily.

"Lily! Get that thing away from me!" Mom's scream echoes through the cave. A man coming out pushes past me.

"*Sumimasen,*" we say in unison.

"What is this place?" Dylan asks.

"Watch out! Snake!" I yell. Dylan jumps.

"Jerk!" he says while shaking it off. Works every time.

"Mom, look closely; the spider has red spots on its belly," Lily observes.

"Honestly, Lily," Mom admonishes.

"Keep moving, Jacob," Dad says.

"Are we almost there?" I ask him.

"Yes, yes," Dad responds.

And then we reach it. More candles appear and reveal a small waterfall at the end of the cave. The pool at the bottom of the falls has wicker baskets floating around in it. I watch a woman throw a pile of cash and coins into one of the baskets. She then rinses the basket in the water like she's panning for gold. Once she seems satisfied it's clean, she takes the sopping wet money out of the basket and puts it back in her pocket, claps her hands together, bows, and heads out of the cave.

"Here, Jacob." Dad hands me a big wad of cash. This may be the first time in my life Dad has willingly given me a bunch of money. As I wash my cash in the waterfall, I see an older woman who has lost a grip on her basket. It's floating farther from her and over toward me. I reach to grab her basket, but my hand slips and dumps all the coins into the water.

"*Sumimasen!*" I say. It's my go-to word.

"I got it," Lily yells. She jumps into the waist-deep river and starts to scoop up all the coins that have fallen to the bottom. A group has gathered around to watch what they assume can only be a crazy gaijin kid stealing people's dropped change. The old lady is laughing and clapping her hands in enjoyment.

"Lily, get out of the water," Mom instructs.

"There is a lot of change down here," Lily says. She has filled the woman's basket to the top. She hands it back to the laughing lady, who tries to catch her breath long enough to say thank you.

"There's still more. You want some, Jacob?" Lily asks as she reaches back into the water.

"Lily, for the last time—get out!" Mom is angry. Or embarrassed. Or both.

Lily climbs out of the water and shakes like a wet dog. As we gather up our things and head out of the cave, I shove the soaking cash into my back pocket. By the time we exit out of the darkness and back into the courtyard, there is a group of people whispering and pointing. It would seem the rumours of the thieving gaijins travelled out of the cave faster than we did.

Mom is bowing and apologizing left and right. Dad is frantically typing something on his phone. "What are you doing?" I ask him.

"Drafting an apology in my translator app," he replies. Then he climbs on top of a large rock and holds his phone up high in the air. He touches a button, and it starts talking in Japanese. I look for a place to hide, but a crowd has gathered to listen. A few people begin to laugh; others walk away, and a young woman gives Lily a beach towel to dry off.

"What did you say?" I ask him.

"Sorry," he says.

"That sounded like a lot more than sorry," I say.

"Well, there may have been a part about your sister's inappropriate behaviour," he says.

"What? What did you say?" I am dying to know what he said about Lily. "What's the Japanese word for crazy?" I continue. He ignores me.

"Team, time to go," Dad instructs.

"But . . ." Lily protests.

"Now, Lily Elizabeth," Mom warns. Lily gives the towel back to the young woman, and we work our way toward the path.

"Jacob, can I have my money back?" Dad asks with his hand stretched out.

"But . . ." I drop the wet money into his hand.

Dylan tosses another coin into a small fountain. He claps his hands and bows.

"What are you doing?" Mom asks under her breath.

"Making amends," says Dylan. He must have done something right because I saw a monk smile as we headed into the forest.

• • •

"I promised you ice cream, didn't I?" Dad says, between bites.

"And you delivered," Mom replies.

We are sitting on a crowded beach eating ice cream. Dylan and Lily have taken their shoes off and are splashing in the surf with some other kids.

I send Yuki a quick text: little girl swimming emoji, money emoji, buddha emoji.

She texts back: "??"

"I'll explain later," I answer.

Dad sits next to me. "You know, if you head across that water right now and just keep going, you'll eventually hit Seattle."

"I miss Seattle," I say.

"Me too, kid. But I found you a beach, right? Isn't it great?!" He holds his arms out wide and points at the busy stretch of shoreline.

"It is a beach," I replied.

"And we washed our money today at the shrine, and if we're lucky, we'll get back five times the amount we washed." He picks up some garbage and heads over to the trash.

I take a bite of my ice cream and a deep breath of ocean air. It may not be a Pacific Northwest ocean breeze, but it is from the Pacific, and I can taste the salt in the air. I bend down to grab my backpack and see a wet 5,000 yen bill in the sand by my feet. I turn to Dad, who gives me a wink. I guess washing money temples and this side of the Pacific aren't all bad. I put the 5,000Y in my pocket and go splash in the water with the twins. Not a total waste of a weekend.

CHAPTER NINE

Tsuku Tsuku Boshi

WE ARE AT the park waiting for Mom as she shops. I have to give it to the Japanese. The same way they somehow built a port-a-potty on a tiny square plot of land, they have managed to master the art of city parks. There are trees and green spaces every couple of blocks. No space goes to waste. Where there is a foot or two, they plant a tree.

Last week Dylan and I spent a whole morning climbing a (human-made) waterfall and catching (stocked) fish a few blocks from our apartment. For a brief moment, it felt like we were home again. This time as we linger in the park, we aren't playing baseball or climbing a waterfall but watching a group of local kids as they collect giant beetle-like bugs called cicadas (or "semi" in Japanese) to keep as pets. We have cicadas in Washington, but nobody keeps them as pets.

Lily can barely contain herself. "They spend their lives underground and then make a tunnel to reach the surface. Isn't it cool?"

She stops and realizes she isn't going to get any reaction from us, so she heads off in search of other future entomologists, the technical term for someone crazy enough to want to spend their lives studying bugs.

Lily is running up and down the park stairway, talking to every kid about cicada trapping. I am pretty confident most of them don't speak English, but that's not stopping Lily. She carries in one hand a small plastic Hello Kitty® collection box in hopes that Mom will let her take one home. Fat chance.

Dylan and I are sitting on a bench, watching the chaos ensue. "It says here some species of cicadas have a high-pitched scream that can exceed over 100 denticles," Dylan reads from his phone.

"You mean decibels?" I correct him.

"Yeah, decibels; wait, what's a decibel?" Dylan asks.

"One hundred decibels, that's as loud as Lily screaming," I say.

"Wow," he responds.

"Yeah. There is no way Mom is letting her take one home," I tell him. We both nod and quietly laugh to ourselves. Poor Lily. She has been waiting for the cicada season since we moved to Tokyo.

"*Tsuku-tsuku boshi. Tsuku-tsuku boshi*," calls Lily as she runs over to us. She plops herself on the bench. "That's the sound they make. Can you hear it?"

"Umm, no; it just sounds like a bunch of screaming to me," I say.

"I think I hear it," says Dylan as he leans his head to the side and concentrates on the loud sound of the thousands of bugs.

"Did you know that in Japan, insects are like heroes?" Lily asks.

"No," I reply.

"What do you mean?" Dylan asks.

"Have you ever noticed that all those comic books you like so much have beetles as superheroes?" she says to Dylan.

"I guess there's that samurai guy who looks like a beetle," he says.

"Yeah, that's a rhinoceros beetle," she says and gives me a know-it-all smile. "And what about grasshoppers? They show up in all your anime," she continues.

"I guess so," Dylan says.

"The Japanese love pet bugs. I heard they have a whole section in the pet store just for bugs," she says.

"No way Mom is going to let you get a pet bug," I tell her.

"Pfft," she snorts.

Suddenly, a Japanese boy is standing in front of us. He is wearing a yellow hat, a neatly tucked-in shirt, and grey shorts. He holds a Totoro plastic collection box with sticks and leaves carefully placed inside, waiting for its prisoner.

"*Tsuku-tsuku boshi. Tsuku-tsuku boshi,*" he repeats, smiling at Lily. They chant together as they skip away in search of an unsuspecting cicada to trap. I unwrap a stick of my Pepperfruits gum and offer a piece to Dylan.

"No, thanks. I don't know how you can eat that stuff. Why would anyone put pepper in gum?" says a disgusted Dylan.

"Because it's awesome," I tell him.

"You're turning Japanese!" he jokes. He says this every time I defend some strange Japanese food or habit. He doesn't know it's all part of my All-Star Expat plan. I've discovered

Pepperfruit gum and an energy drink called Pocari Sweat, but there is no way I am going to love some eardrum-bursting, cockroach-like flying beetle.

At last, Mom is here. "Mom, did you find marshmallows?"

"Yes, I did, Jacob. Your teeth will be full of sugar bugs tomorrow," she replies with a wink.

"Umm . . . those may not be the only bugs in the house," warns Dylan as we all watch Lily skip towards us with a look of pure joy on her face and a plastic container that is singing: "*Tsuku-tsuku boshi. Tsuku-tsuku boshi.*"

"What does she have?" Mom is squinting to see what Lily's holding.

"Nothing, Mom," I hastily reply and push Dylan aside.

"Follow my lead," I whisper to him.

"Lily, do you hear the bugs in the trees?" I yell as I stand between her and Mom.

"I hear them!" Dylan says a little too loudly. Mom looks up.

"In the trees. Do you hear the bugs?" I yell at Lily again.

"Um, yeah," she calls out and holds up her container.

"In the trees, Lily," I warn her. "Can you hear them? In. The. Trees?" There is only so much I can give away with my look before she reaches Mom. I am moving my eyes from the container to the trees, to Mom, to the container, to the trees. Lily gets the message and slowly moves the box behind her back as she approaches us.

"Those bugs in the trees are really loud," she says to Mom the moment she reaches us.

"Yes, I guess they are," Mom replies, "and what's behind your back, Lily?"

"It's just a collection box. I found some lovely rocks and twigs," Lily sweetly replies. "And look," she adds with some girly charm, "a flower."

51

She reaches down and picks the first brightly coloured weed within reach and hands it to Mom. "For you." Lily smiles again.

"Oh, thank you, sweetie," Mom gushes like putty in our hands.

Dylan continues to ask Mom pointed questions about her groceries and quickens their pace to give Lily and me some privacy as we start up the long flight of stairs out of the park.

"Dear, those bugs are loud." Mom is looking all around her. It's the last thing we hear before they are out of earshot.

"Keep that bug out of sight," I warn Lily.

"Thank you, Jacob. Thank you." She comes in for a hug. I pull away but let her lean in for a side hug.

"No problem."

"Where should I keep it?"

"Don't know."

"Maybe in my bedroom near the window. Mom will think it's in the tree outside," she suggests.

"Good plan."

"Oh, thank you, Jacob." She leans in for another side hug, but I step away. I can't wait to see how this plays out when Mom discovers we have a pet screaming cockroach.

CHAPTER TEN

Akihabara

"JACOB HAS A girlfriend! Jacob has a girlfriend!" sings Lily.

"Give it up, Lily!" I yell.

"Ohhh. Someone's very defensive," Lily replies.

"Defensive about what?" asks Dylan.

"About your guuurlfriend!" says Lily.

"Give it up, Lily!" I warn her.

"What girlfriend?" Dylan asks.

"That girl from the baseball diamond," Lily replies.

"What? She's your girlfriend?" Dylan asks.

"No!"

Mom walks in with her book in hand. "What's going on in here?"

"Jacob has a girlfriend. He's going on a date today!" Lily says.

"I'm just meeting my friend. You are so immature!" I bark back.

"OK, Lily, that's enough," Mom says. "I got no sleep last night. Those stupid bugs in the trees won't stop screaming. I swear there is one living in my bedroom. Jacob, when will you be back?"

"I don't know," I say.

"Well, where are you going?" she asks.

"An arcade," I say.

"I want to go!" yells Dylan.

"Remember, Dylan, today is your first sumi-e class," says Mom.

"What? Jacob's going to an arcade, and I have to go to a swimming class?" Dylan whines.

"No, sumi-e," Mom says.

"What the heck is sumi?" Dylan asks.

Mom ignores him and continues to drill me with questions. Dylan doesn't know that I convinced Mom to sign him up for sumi-e, traditional Japanese calligraphy painting, because he "really seemed interested."

"Who is this friend you are going with?" she asks.

"Yuki," I reply.

"Jacob has a girlfriend. Jacob has a girlfriend!" Lily starts again. Dylan is busy looking up "sumi-e" on his phone.

"Mom, I'm leaving," I say as I glare at Lily.

"Do you have your phone?" she asks.

"Yes," I reply.

"Wait. Stop. Do you hear that? It's that screaming bug again. Can anyone else hear that?" Mom asks.

"No," we all reply in unison.

"How can I get any work done with that horrible noise?!" Mom yells. Mom helps people with taxes. She is still doing work for her Seattle clients and is working from the apartment. I can imagine the sound of that bug drilling in her head all day is about as painful as when Mom tries to explain to me how she "maximizes someone's tax benefits."

"Jacob, are you sure you know where you're going?" Mom asks.

"Yes," I reply. "It's only a few stops on the subway."

"What?" She stomps her foot in a mother-like move and calls for Dad. He comes out of the kitchen, coffee in hand. "You need to take Jacob to the arcade to meet his friend."

"Mom, I can do it on my own," I beg.

"You are not old enough to take a subway on your own," she says.

"Yes, I am," I argue.

"Sure, he is," says Dad.

Mom gives him a look.

He turns to me. "Sorry, kid, I'll have to take you. Give me a minute." He disappears upstairs.

"Mom! Is this sumi-e?" Dylan holds up his phone and shows us a black-and-white picture of a painted flower. He looks amazed and disgusted. I try hard to avoid eye contact, or I'll burst out laughing.

Once again, Mom ignores him and keeps on me. "Be home by five. We're going out for dinner tonight."

"The ramen place with the crazy obaasan?" I ask. She doesn't respond, which means yes.

"I want you to be nice to Yoshioka san. She has offered to give you some cooking lessons," Mom says.

Could this morning get any worse?

"OK, let's go," calls Dad from the front door.

"Fine. Whatever." I follow him.

Mom starts again, "Jacob. I—" I don't hear the rest. My headphones are already on, and I can't get out the door fast enough. Yuki is my first friend in Tokyo, and Lily just made it weird.

Tonight I'll have to sit on the tatami floor in the ramen place and listen to never-ending questions about my new girlfriend, who isn't even my girlfriend. All the while making sure I don't make any gaijin mistakes and get karate chopped by a crazy old lady who is now apparently my cooking teacher.

We are swiftly walking toward the subway when Dad pulls off my headphones.

"Jacob."

"Yeah?"

"You know the Japanese subway system is one of the cleanest, safest, and most efficient subway systems in the world," he says, "and we've been on it a bunch of times already."

"Right." I am not in the mood for another chapter out of his Japanese guidebook.

"Do you know where you're going?" he asks.

"Yeah. Yuki gave me directions."

He stops walking. "Then you don't need me to babysit."

I look up to see we are standing across the street from the subway.

"Be careful," he says. "Your mom will kill me if you get lost."

"Thank you. Thank you. Thank you." Finally, someone gets that I'm not a baby anymore. I give him a big hug.

"Text me when you get there." I nod in agreement and run across the street to the subway.

I pull out Yuki's directions: "Take the blue line to Akihabara stop. Take the south exit. Meet me in front of McDonald's." I look up at the giant subway map. I live on the blue line, so my station should be on the same line as Akihabara, but the map has over twenty-five coloured lines—and several different shades of blue—all going in random directions. There is no east to west. There are no mountains, oceans, or landmarks to point me in the right direction. Even if I did figure it out, I have no idea how to use the ticket machine. Maybe Mom was right. I look across the street; Dad has already left.

"Lost?" a man asks from beside me. He looks a little younger than Dad, is wearing a dark blue suit, and carries an umbrella. It's ninety degrees out, and the sun is shining. Why the umbrella? He moves closer to me and looks up at the map.

"I'm OK," I reply. Mom rule #1: Don't talk to strangers. I keep staring at the map.

"Lost?" he asks again.

"No, I'm OK," I reply shortly. I look down at my directions from Yuki. He edges closer to me and looks at my paper.

"Akihabara?" he reads.

"Yes," I reply.

"Ah-so, come, come." He is ushering me toward the ticket machines. I tried to get rid of this stranger twice, but he is determined to help me. He taps on a few keys, touches the screen a couple of times, points to the station name, and says, "Akihabara?" I nod my head. He looks at me strangely, then reaches into his pocket, pulls out some coins, and buys me a ticket.

"Come, come." He ushers me toward the ticket gate and takes me to a track.

"Akihabara," he says. Then he counts on his hands to six and holds his fingers up for me.

"Six stops?" I ask.

"Hi, hi," the stranger says.

The train on the opposite side arrives, and he looks over at it, checks his watch, fumbles with his umbrella, looks at me, and lets the train pass.

"Was that your train?" I ask him. He dismissively waves his hand at me and continues to wait. I think he just missed his train to make sure I got on mine. I reach into my pocket and pull out some change to pay him back; again, he dismissively waves his hand at me.

My train arrives; he holds up his six fingers again and says, "Akihabara," and bows slightly. He still hasn't broken eye contact as I get on the train. The warning sound for the closing doors beeps, and he turns away and heads over to the other side of the tracks. I'm so in the moment that I almost forget to thank him, but I yell, "Thank you!" just as the door shuts. I see him whip his head around and smile.

There is a group of little girls sitting next to me. Two of them are wearing face masks. I can't believe Mom thinks I need a babysitter when even kindergarteners take the trains alone in Japan. Six stops later, we arrive at Akihabara. I follow the kids off the train and up the staircase towards the south exit. I can't make out what they are saying, but I think I hear the word "*gaijin*" a few times between giggles. I've gotten used to locals talking about me right in my face because they assume I don't understand. Still, every day I pick up a few new words, and soon I'll know everything they are saying. Who will be laughing then?

The kindergarteners and I step out of the subway station, and it is pouring with rain—not the grey, drizzly stuff that you see in Seattle that goes on for months but heavy, torrential, monsoon-like rain. The kind of rain that arrives out of nowhere and makes rivers on sidewalks and lakes in parking lots. I watch the little kids as they casually reach into their backpacks, pull out small umbrellas, hold them over their little heads, and happily walk away. I get soaked in the thirty seconds it takes to jog across the street to McDonald's. Kinders–1, Jacob–0.

"Did you have any trouble getting here?" Yuki asks.

"No, it was easy," I reply while wringing out the bottom of my shirt.

"I see," she says. "No umbrella?"

"How was I supposed to know a monsoon was coming?" I ask.

"It rains every day in June and July," she says.

"Every day?" I ask.

"Yeah, just for a bit," she says. "You need to carry an umbrella." She taps her backpack and smiles. "Ready for the arcade?"

"You lead the way," I say. "I'm done with directions for today."

I follow Yuki and quickly pull out my phone to text Dad: "Made it."

He texts back: "Good."

I reply: "Should have brought an (umbrella emoji)."

He replies, "Me too (and sends a picture of wet shoes)."

I look up from my phone and stop dead in my tracks. Two minutes in Akihabara, and I realize my parents know nothing about Japan. I have been in Tokyo for almost two months now, and I've seen tea ceremonies, temples, and tatami. I have sat through lectures at dinner on sumo, samurai, and sumi-e. My parents think that Japan is living in some old world, a black-and-white movie.

Akihabara is nothing like that. It's loud, colourful, and crowded. The businessmen are bumping up against teens dressed as anime characters. Just within a block, 300 screens are playing video games, ads, and music videos. The storefronts sell electronic animals next to VR games, collector vinyl toys, and manga. I've seen crowds and chaos but nothing like this. Akihabara is the Tokyo I've been waiting to see. Dylan is going to freak out when I tell him about this place.

Yuki opens her arms wide. "Welcome to Akihabara."

"*Sugoi*! Where's the arcade?" I ask Yuki.

"A few blocks," she replies. "But you can try all sorts of games inside the stores."

She pulls me out from under the awning and into the next storefront. The shop has every kind of manga imaginable. We play an old-school fishing arcade game for half an hour before the shopkeeper tells us to move on.

A man on the street is handing out manga samples with comic drawings of nude girls on the cover. They appear to be in full combat with a giant fish. Yuki takes one, shrugs, and puts it in her bag.

"They just hand those out?" I ask.

"It's a manga," she replies.

"Yeah, I know what manga is, but isn't it strange to hand out THAT KIND of manga to kids on the street?" I ask. She looks at me and rolls her eyes.

"Look at it," she says, showing it to me. "Just some girls defending the world and kicking butt. No big deal. Totally normal in Japan," she explains. "Americans are so easily offended."

"Can I have it?" I ask.

"Sure," she says and gives it to me. I stuff it in my back pocket. It may be normal in Japan to have comic books with naked people, but Mom will have a total fit when she finds it in Dylan's top drawer.

"Let's grab a bite to eat," Yuki suggests. She heads into a convenience store. The door chimes, "Irasshaimase," and I take a moment to look around. Once again, I realize my parents have been keeping me from some of Tokyo's best secrets. This convenience store has restaurant-quality lunches. There are two aisles of perfectly packaged lunch boxes.

"Awesome, they have bento boxes," I say to Yuki.

"You know that bento means box?" she says.

"So I'm calling them box boxes?" I ask.

She laughs. "Yeah, sort of."

"OK, they have bento," I correct myself.

"Yeah, but we're not getting bento," she tells me. "We're getting nikuman."

"What?" I ask.

She grabs a drink, cold coffee, and I get a Pocari Sweat. We head over to the cashier. She points to a small oven that sits on the counter and asks the cashier for two nikuman.

"What is nikuman?" I ask.

"Just try it." She hands me a small bag with a piping hot bun inside.

"There are no fish erasers in here, are there?" I ask.

"What?" she looks confused.

"Nothing," I reply.

We sit on the sidewalk and pull out our nikuman. It's a steamed pork bun, like a giant dim sum, and it tastes incredible. I could eat three more.

"I'm getting another," I tell Yuki and head back in. As I'm standing at the counter, I see another little oven next to the nikuman, labelled Pizzaman." Enough said.

I squat back on the sidewalk next to Yuki and pull out my Pizzaman, a giant steamed pizza bun. Weird, yes, but still better than any actual pizza I've had in Tokyo.

Yuki points across the street at a large building with ten-foot posters of anime characters hanging from the windows. "Last stop before the arcade, my favourite store. It has ten floors of nothing but manga."

We head into the store. Yuki starts to run up the stairs. "Go check out floor nine!" she yells back to me. I take my time checking out all the floors before landing on nine. I see Yuki elbow deep in a stack of comic books in the corner. She has put on some headphones and looks like she is settling in for a while.

I casually look around and don't see anything I recognize. I pick up a magazine and start to flip through the pages. Girly. I pick up another one. Girly. I feel someone breathing on my neck. I turn around to see three girls dressed in full Sailor Moon costumes, and they don't look happy. I take a step back, and they inch closer to me. Another step back. Another step closer. I quickly look to see if Yuki notices, but she is completely immersed in her reading. I whip my head around to see if anyone else notices, but all I see are more girls. Everywhere girls. Girls shopping. Girls reading. Girls giggling. Girls in the magazines. Girl toys. Girl posters. I start to panic. "Yuki!" I call across the room. She doesn't hear me. I try to reach her, but the Sailor Moon trio has me backed up against the wall. I try again, yelling, "Yuki!" No answer.

The girls are pushing me towards the stairs. Are they going to push me down the stairs? Is this it for me? Couldn't I at least be taken out by the guy from *Black Butler*? Seriously. When we reach the top of the staircase, the girls move aside. Right in front of me is a giant sign with a stick figure of a girl and a stick figure of a boy. The boy has a giant X over his body.

"Yuki?" I call from the stairway. No answer. Dylan will never believe me when I tell him I got kicked out of an all-girl manga store by Sailor Moon.

It takes about fifteen minutes for Yuki to find me sitting in the stairway. "Where did you go?" she asks.

"I think this is a girls-only floor," I say.

"Well, isn't that obvious by the sign? I told you to go to floor seven," she says.

"No, you said nine," I reply.

"No, I said nana—that's seven," she explains.

"In Japanese maybe, but it sure sounded like nine in English," I say. Now she is apologizing but also laughing at her mistake. I tell her the whole story.

"I had no idea Sailor Moon was so badass," I say.

"Sailor Moon is totally badass."

By the time we reach the arcade, I have already seen so much that a stadium-sized arcade filled with every type of racing, dancing, and fighting game you can think of seems the least exciting part of the day. I successfully rode a train on my own, discovered where the Tokyo youth hang out was, played tons of games, had my first nikuman, got bullied by Sailor Moon, and made a great friend. Tokyo isn't stuck in the 1800s with Mom and Dad; it is wild, loud, crazy, and I think I might like it.

CHAPTER ELEVEN

The Cooking Lesson

"I HEAR IT again," Mom says while buttering her toast, stabbing and massacring the bread like the toast itself has been screaming, "*Tsuku boshi!*" for days.

"I know those bloody bugs are outside, but why does it sound like one is nesting in my ear?" she continues.

I almost tossed Lily's pet cicada myself. Twice. Tsuku (yes, she named it) hasn't stopped screaming since we hid it in Lily's room. My want for the bug to stop crying is only outweighed by how awesome it will be when Mom discovers it.

"I can't hear it," I lie to Mom.

"How can you not hear that?" Mom insists. Now she eats her buttered toast by tearing it into tiny pieces and chewing hard. Lily comes into the kitchen, singing to herself.

"Lily, when do these bugs return underground?" Mom barks.

"What bugs?" Lily asks.

"The screaming ones!"

"Oh, they only live for about six weeks above ground. They mate, lay eggs, and then die."

"Then die . . . die . . ." Mom repeats as she takes her cup of coffee and heads into the living room.

The moment Mom is out of earshot, Lily jumps closer to me. "Do you think she knows?"

"I don't think so."

"Should I move Tsuku somewhere else?"

"Where?"

"I don't know. The TV room?"

"No way!"

"I'm going to open a few windows to drown out the sound," Lily decides and heads upstairs.

Mom reappears. "Jacob, get dressed. Today's your first cooking lesson with Yoshioka san."

"Do I have to?"

"Yes," she insists. Mom and Dad are getting back at me for the chopstick incident by making me take cooking lessons from the crazy old lady.

"Oh, I forgot to tell you. Haru is going to meet you there. He's going to help translate for his grandmother," Mom says.

"You know he might push me into a vat of piping hot ramen after his obaasan karate chops me," I say back.

"What are you talking about?"

"Nothing."

Have you ever seen the movie *Karate Kid*? Me neither. But I know there is a scene where some kid gets tricked into doing a bunch of chores, thinking he is training to become a karate master. This is how I picture my cooking lessons with Yoshioka san. I walk to the ramen shop, and as I enter the restaurant, I let the curtain on the door slide over my shoulders and wait for "Irashaimase," but it doesn't come. Instead, Haru is in front of me.

"Ohayo, good morning," he says.

"Ohayo," I reply. He smiles.

"Obaasan has given us a list of things to buy. I will get some money from her. You sweep." He hands me a broom and disappears behind the kitchen.

I don't want to anger Obaasan, so I start to sweep even though the floors already look clean. A man comes to the door and drops off a box of vegetables. He looks at me strangely, bows, and backs his way out the door without breaking eye contact. I keep sweeping the clean floors. Another person pops their head in the door, smiles, and backs out. Then another.

"Ladies and gentlemen, step right up; the sweeping gaijin attraction is now open," I call out to the empty room. Then Haru appears.

"You are sweeping," he says.

"Well, you told me to."

"I was kidding; what do you think this is—*Karate Kid?*" he says. "*Ikimashou.*"

"What does that mean?"

"It means let's go."

"*Ikimashou,*" I repeat and off we go.

Haru is loading leeks, green onions, carrots, potatoes, and what looks like giant radish into his basket. I am admiring a mango with a 550Y price tag.

"We don't put mango in ramen," Haru says.

"550Y, that's like five bucks for a mango," I say.

"We don't put mango in ramen," he says again. I follow his gaze and see a couple of American kids in the next aisle. They are playing catch with one of the perfectly wrapped apples.

One kid is pretending to be the catcher while the other is pitching. Everyone in the store sees them, some people shake their heads in disappointment, but no one says anything.

I point at the boys and ask Haru, "Why doesn't someone say something?"

"Just ignore them," Haru says.

"But they're rude," I argue.

"No one wants to start or cause scene."

"But they already started something by playing catch with the produce."

"Just ignore it." Haru is getting frustrated, and I realize he is more concerned with me causing a scene than with the boys playing catch in a grocery store. Just like Yuki told me at the baseball diamond, no one is to stand apart from the team. We are all meant to live in some kind of peaceful harmony. Haru doesn't want me to embarrass him. Well, I am embarrassed to be American for the first time since arriving in Tokyo because of these two kids. I can't just sit back and let a couple of idiots make us all look bad.

I walk over to the boys and intercept their pass, put the apple back on the counter, and turn to the boy who threw the apple. "Look, if you want to improve your pitch, why don't you go practice with a real ball somewhere else?"

"What did you say?" he asks me and moves a step closer to me.

"I said it's going to take more than tossing an apple to improve your weak pitch."

He takes another step closer to me. He's at least a foot shorter than me (I know because I checked before entering into this.). I see Haru out of the corner of my eye; he is leaning forward, trying to hear what's going on without getting too close. The cashier has also stopped what he is doing and is watching us closely.

"Just go play somewhere else. You are ruining the harmony of this store," I say.

"What?"

"Go somewhere else," I warn them again.

"Carter, let's go," the other guy says and pushes his friend towards the door.

"See you on the field, Chester," I called to him.

"It's Carter," he barks back.

"Whatever, Chester," I reply. He turns to give me a dirty look and walks out.

Haru comes and stands next to me. He picks up the mango I was admiring earlier.

"You like mangoes?" he asks me.

"Of course," I replied.

"For you," he says and puts the overpriced mango in his basket.

Haru is in the kitchen rambling off in Japanese to his obaasan. She has her back to me, but I can tell she is listening intently. I can only assume he's telling her all about the grocery store incident since she keeps glancing back at me and smiling. I unpack the vegetables and place them on the kitchen counter as instructed. Just as I finish, Obaasan walks over and sets a plate in front of me. It is the mango Haru selected. She slices the mango and makes it into a fan shape. In the middle of the fan is a strawberry cut like a flower. She pushes a stool toward the counter for me. Haru hops on a seat next to me and puts down his plate with perfectly sliced mango. He doesn't have a strawberry flower, and I wonder if he ate it already or if there is only one for me, the boy who scared off the obnoxious Americans at the grocery store.

After eating our snack, Haru tells me it is time to start cooking. Obaasan takes a dish towel from a drawer and folds it over a few times, wraps it around her head, and ties it off at the back. She tosses two more dish towels to Haru.

"Follow me," he instructs and starts to fold his towel. I follow as best I can as I don't typically fold clothes. Haru has his cloth securely tied on his head while I am still trying to fold mine into triangles. He takes my towel, wraps it, and fastens it around my head.

"Is this necessary?" I ask.

"Yes," he says.

"Why?"

"Because Obaasan has her ways. Don't argue."

"Oh, I have no intention of arguing with your grandmother. I've seen her karate chop."

"Obaasan."

"Right, Obaasan."

Obaasan pulls some packages out of the fridge and reveals a stack of chicken bones and pork bones. She points to a giant cauldron of boiling water and hands the bones to us.

"We put the bones in the water to boil," Haru tells me. Obaasan starts to give him more instructions in Japanese.

"We are making the soup," Haru says, "the base for the ramen. It's the same in English and Japanese, right? Soup." Haru repeats.

"Soup. Got it."

He digs into the fridge and pulls out a bag of seaweed. It's not the type of seaweed you see wrapped around sushi or the crisp strips you see sprinkled on rice; this looks like the stuff you gather at the beach and throw at your sister. What was once a slimy green mess floating in the ocean was now a dried-up green mess about to swim in our soup.

"*Kombu*," Obaasan says.

"*Kombu*," I repeat.

"Dried seaweed," Haru explains.

"Why?" I ask.

"It gives the famous Japanese umami flavour," Haru says. I don't know what that is, but I nod my head. I'll look it up later.

"*Katsuobushi*," Obaasan says. She opens a jar and reveals some other dried, fishy-smelling thing. It's pink and flakey, and it stinks.

"*Katsuobushi*," I repeat while trying not to gag. It smells like cat food.

"Umm," Haru is searching for the English word. "Tuna!" he says.

"Ah, dried tuna," I say. Haru nods and helps Obaasan shake the tuna flakes into the soup. Obaasan is now adding spices in unmarked tins and isn't sharing this part of the recipe. She says something to Haru.

"We are done," Haru says.

"What, we put some things in a pot. What about the rest of it?"

"We need to cook soup all night. Tomorrow, we make tare."

"What is tare?"

"It makes the flavour."

"Can we make it now?" I ask.

"*Dewa mata ashita*," says Obaasan, as she is pushing me out of the kitchen.

"See you tomorrow," Haru says and gestures towards the door.

"What about all the vegetables we bought?" I ask.

"They are for dinner tonight," he says.

"What?"

"*Dewa mata ashita*," Obaasan says.

"OK, OK, Obaasan. *Arigato*. See you tomorrow," I say.

"See you tomorrow," says Haru.

It is a short walk home, but I take the time to imagine what those extra spices might be. Salt? Mom always salts her soups. Pepper? Maybe it needs a kick. Some other kind of dried-up fish? I sure hope it's not shredded-up fish erasers. I turn the corner to the apartment building, and there is Lily, an empty collection box in hand and tears streaming down her face.

"Oh no! I missed it!" I yell.

"I . . . I know, Jacob, I'll miss Tsuku too," she says between sobs.

"Nooo—I missed it. What did Mom say? How did she find Tsuku? Was she super pissed? Are you grounded?"

"I hate you, Jacob!" she screams and runs back inside.

"Come on, let's go get a Caplis, and I'll tell you all about it," says Dylan. I didn't even notice he was sitting right next to Lily.

"Sure," I say.

"But first, are you going to take that stupid towel off your head?" he asks.

● ● ●

Day two of the ramen lesson. Haru is once again waiting for me just inside the restaurant. He seems impressed to see I have already tied on my cloth headscarf. He doesn't need to know that Mom put it on for me.

"Are we buying your dinner groceries today?" I ask.

"No," Haru says, "but you can help unpack the delivery." Just then, the delivery guy drops off the vegetables and smiles as he backs away. When I go to pick up the box, I notice a mango sitting on top.

"The delivery guy is also the owner of the grocery store we were in yesterday," says Haru. "You are famous." He grabs the mango from the top of the box, takes a step back, and tosses it to me.

As we play a light game of catch with my favourite fruit, I can't help but wonder how this kid pushed me over at the park so long ago.

"Haru?" I ask.

"Hi," he responds.

"I've wanted to ask you about the time we first met."

"Hi," he responds as he quickly checks over his shoulder to see if Obaasan is within earshot.

"Why did you push me over?" I ask. He looks at me, his eyebrows raised and eyes wide open. I continue. "I mean, I know I made fun of your Giants T-shirt." I toss him the mango.

"I did not push you over. Your brother did," he says. He stops the game of catch. His face is bright red, and he's breathing fast. He squeezes the mango so hard that I think the juice is starting to drip out. It appears he is more embarrassed to tattle on Dylan than he would be if he did it himself.

"Dylan did it?" I ask.

"Your brother. Yes."

I think about it, then nod. "That makes sense." I hold out my hand, encouraging him to toss the mango. He throws it to me.

"Why did you run?" I ask as I toss it back.

"Haru san. Jacob san," yells Obaasan from the kitchen. Haru takes a step closer to me and whispers under his breath. "Broken tap. Very bad. We were never in the park."

"Right. We were never in the park." I nod in agreement. So he ran to not get in trouble, that I get, and I have great respect for a guy who would rather take the blame than be a snitch, but it's payback time for Dylan—time to dig out that nude manga and put it in his drawer.

"It is time to cook," says Haru. He helps me carry the box of food to the kitchen counter. Obaasan looks at my head and nods in approval. She tosses a fresh towel to Haru, and he wraps up his head. She starts talking in Japanese.

"Today we make tare," Haru translates.

"Right, the flavour," I say.

Haru pauses while Obaasan keeps talking. You can see him trying to translate in his head, and I wonder if my Japanese will ever be that good. We studied Spanish back home, but my friends and I used that class to trade baseball cards. I think learning Japanese is more important at this point.

"Sorry, my Obaasan talks too much. This tare is a Tokyo-style tare. It has a soy sauce flavour. Ramen from other parts of Japan, like Hokkaido in the north and Sapporo in the south, have different tare. She says her special tare recipe is very old, like her. My grandfather made the recipe after the war when they opened this restaurant. He uses Tokyo style, but he is from the south, so he has a secret south flavour that makes his tare special," Haru explains.

He takes a deep breath and rolls his eyes at me. I am guessing he has heard this story many times. Trust me; I get it. My dad's uncle with the missing finger. That guy only has one story, and he loves to tell it.

"Ginger, garlic, green onion," Haru says as he places food in front of me. We start to peel, chop, and grate.

"Mirin, sake, soya," says Obaasan, and she places three bottles in front of me. I take a good sniff of the mirin, the soy, then I reach for the sake, and Obaasan swiftly picks it up. She wags her finger at me.

"Sake is alcohol," Haru says.

"I was just going to smell it," I reply.

Obaasan starts pouring the liquids into the bowl, where we have put the diced garlic, green onion, and ginger. She then tips it all into a pot, adds some more secret spices, and boils it. It smells fantastic—sweet, salty, garlicky. She removes the pan from the stovetop and claps her hands together.

"*Dewa mata ashita*," Obaasan says. This time I don't argue.

"See you tomorrow," I reply and turn to leave.

"Wait, Jacob," says Haru, "Tomorrow, we finish the ramen."

"OK."

"And we eat," he adds with a wink.

● ● ●

"I am going to the park!" Lily declares.

"Not alone, you're not," Mom tells her. The two haven't stopped fighting since Tsuku was discovered, decimated, and discarded.

"I hate you. I hate you, Mom," Lily boldly states.

"Great. I'll put that on a cake."

"You would?" Lily asks.

"I would," Mom replies.

"What is going on here?" Dad says as he enters the room. He is dressed for work and about to make his great escape.

"Mom won't let me go to the park," Lily complains.

"Jacob, can you take Lily to the park?" Dad asks.

"Sorry, Dad. I'm off to my cooking lesson." I grab my dish towel headscarf and run for the door. I can hear Dad calling for Dylan as I slam the front door shut. Dylan will be stuck at the park with Lily for hours looking for bugs and will be home just in time to get in trouble for the nude manga I put in his drawer.

Haru isn't waiting for me when I arrive this time.

"Haru? Yoshioka san? Obaasan?" I call out. Nothing. I tie on the headscarf. All-Star Expat. I pick up the broom and start sweeping the clean floors. My vegetable friend arrives with his delivery. This time he brings me a nashi.

"*Arigato!*" I thank him and take a big bite. It is crunchy and tart like a green apple but with the consistency of a pear.

"Delicious," I say.

"*Oishi*," says a voice behind me. It is Haru. "It means delicious."

"*Oishi*," I say to my friend. He bows and again backs out the door.

"Are you ready to make ramen?" Haru asks.

"Absolutely," I say between bites.

Obaasan digs into the fridge and pulls out containers filled with all the things we have been making. She strains all of the bones and various dried fish things out of the soup and pours it back into a giant pot to reheat. She takes the tare out of the fridge and sets it aside and pulls out a large chunk of cooked pork. It looks like it has been marinating in some brown sauce.

"What is the pork marinating in?" I ask Haru.

"A soy sauce marinade, kind of like the tare we made," he replies. Obaasan starts giving Haru directions, and he is pulling things out of the fridge and handing them to me: soft-boiled eggs marinating in the sauce, thin noodles, green onions, mushrooms, and something pickled. Haru informs me that it is bamboo shoots. Then things start to move fast. Obaasan is thinly slicing the pork into little discs. Haru is boiling the noodles in water.

"Why are we working so fast?" I ask Haru.

"Ramen must be eaten hot. Boiling," he explains.

"*Boru*," Obaasan barks at me.

"What?" I ask.

"Bowls," Haru says.

"*Boru*," barks Obaasan again. Right, bowls, bowls—on the counter are a stack of large bowls. I pull out three and place them on the table. Haru pours some boiling soup into each bowl. Obaasan adds some tare.

"Slice up the green onions," Haru directs. I start to chop the onions.

"Faster," he says.

"OK, OK." I am slicing as fast as I can. Obaasan drains the noodles from the boiling water and splits them up between the three bowls. Haru slices the soft-boiled eggs in half while Obaasan places a handful of dried seaweed on top. Haru arranges some mushrooms and bamboo next to the seaweed. Obaasan adds slices of pork next to the mushrooms and places two egg halves next to them.

"Onions," says Haru. I quickly carry my sliced green onions over to the bowl and place them in the only spot left, the middle. Everyone stops. I look at my dish. It is a piece of art. Haru smiles at me, and I smile back. Obaasan frowns.

"Did I do something wrong?" I ask Haru as sweat drips from my face.

"No," says Haru. "You did great." He is listening to Obaasan, who is talking to herself.

"She says something is missing," Haru says. "Each ramen recipe must be a reflection of its cook. Obaasan says this ramen is not you, Jacob." He rolls his eyes.

I am stunned. I am staring at a bowl of food that I cannot wait to wolf down. How can it not be a reflection of me? I helped cook for three days to make this masterpiece. Obaasan is still frowning. How can I make this ramen mine?

"I got it!" I yell. I run out the front door as fast as I can and straight into the convenience store across the street. I grab my secret ingredient and run back into the kitchen.

"Jacob's Ramen," I say and carefully place a steaming pizza dumpling—a Pizzaman—on top of my perfect ramen. I would have eaten it right away too, but the three of us spent a good ten minutes laughing and taking pictures of our ramen before we dug in.

CHAPTER TWELVE

The Baseball Game

BING! A TEXT. Bing! Another. Bing! And another.

It's seven in the morning! Who's texting me?

"*Jacob.*"

"*Jacob.*"

"*Jacob, you there?*"

It's Yuki. I reply back: "What's up? (sleepy emoji)."

She takes her time responding. I start to doze off again.

Bing! "My dad got tix to the Giants game on the ninth. My brother, dad, and I are going. Three more tickets! You and your brother want to come???? Your sister? Haru?"

Now I'm awake. I text back: "What??? Yes!"

I pause for a moment and imagine Lily at a baseball game.

"I'll bring my brother and Haru."

She replies right away. "Perfect."

"Thanks!"

I'm impressed with how quickly she plans. Well, there is no way I am going back to sleep now. I make myself a bowl of cereal and turn on the TV. A sumo tournament is on.

I've been in Tokyo long enough that I'm starting to like a lot of Japanese things—manga, ramen, tiny parks, vending machine lunches—but I still don't get sumo.

"Morning." It's Dad in his robe. Ever since we moved to Japan, he's started wearing this cotton robe called a yukata around the house. It was pretty weird at first, but now I'm used to it—as long as he doesn't sit with his legs open.

"Are you watching sumo?" he asks as he sits down next to me.

"Yeah, I just don't get it," I reply.

"Well, it's certainly not as popular as baseball, but—" Dad says.

"Baseball!" I interrupt, "Guess what? Yuki got tickets to a Giants game, and she invited me, Dylan, and Haru to come."

"That's so generous," he says.

"I know." I jump off the couch to go wake Dylan. News like this can't wait another minute.

"Aren't you going to finish the sumo match?" Dad asks.

"It's all yours." I toss him the remote.

● ● ●

It's been a long two weeks waiting for the day of the game. Haru, Dylan, and I meet up at the ramen place and head over to the subway to meet Yuki and her family. They are easy to find. Yuki has more Giants gear than an actual player, and her brother is the tallest Japanese kid I've ever seen.

Haru is formally introducing himself to each of them. It is a bit surprising to see how proper Yuki acts when introducing herself and her family. They bow and use drawn-out greetings I don't understand. Once the formal introductions are out of the way, Yuki is back to her usual self, but Haru remains very proper. Thirty minutes and two trains later, we are on our final train change with a swarm of Giants fans.

"It is only two stops from here," Yuki yells to me above the crowd.

"Why is it so crowded?" I call back.

"We are very close to the stadium," she says.

"Doesn't anyone drive to the game?" I ask. It must have been a stupid question because her dad starts to laugh.

"Stay together," her dad instructs. Dylan grabs my hand for the first time in five years, and I let him. The swarm of Giants fans is moving towards the subway. A police officer is standing by each door. I feel relieved someone is here to keep order. He remains still as a train arrives and people start to push and shove.

"Isn't the officer going to help direct traffic?" I ask Yuki, who is now only inches from my face as the crowd squishes us.

"He's not an officer," she replies.

"What is he?"

"He's here to help get more people on the train."

"What do you mean?"

"You'll see."

I watch from our place in line. We are too far back to make it on the first train. The alarm starts to warn that the doors are getting ready to close, and suddenly, the officer, or whatever he is, begins to push people into the train like he is packing meat into a taco. Shoving and pushing bodies into the doorway, forcing people inside the train to smash up against one another and make room for more people. I look at Yuki in disbelief. She smiles and laughs. The door closes, and the train takes off.

We are much closer to the front of the line now, and I fear we are getting on the next train. Yuki's dad starts to pull us closer. I am suddenly jealous of Yuki's brother, whose height lets him see what's going on around him.

"What position does your brother play on his school team?" I ask Yuki.

"Pitcher."

"How come he doesn't play basketball?" I ask. She laughs and gives me that same look that her dad did a moment earlier when I asked about driving to the game. Another stupid question, I guess. The next train pulls in.

"Ready?" her dad asks.

"Ready!" Dylan says. I almost forgot he was there, even though he's holding my hand with a death grip. We start to push our way onto the train. We are stuck somewhere in the middle of the car. I search to find a handle to hold and realize it's not needed; bodies are propping me up, and there is no way I am going to fall over. Then the alarm goes, and the officer starts to push. Arms, legs, faces, and butts are pushing against me. Some kid with a giant foam finger disappears below the crowd, lost in a sea of legs; all that remains is an orange foam finger waving in front of my face. The alarm rings again, and the door closes. Nope. It pops open; there is a limb in the way. Bing! It tries to close again; another arm is stuck. The officer comes closer to the train and gives the people near the door one last push. Bing! The door finally closes, and the train starts.

The train smells like sweat. I can feel sweaty bodies next to me. I taste sweat dripping from my forehead to my mouth. If there is a sound that sweat makes, I hear it.

"We're here!" calls Yuki's dad from somewhere. The door opens, and everyone falls, crawls, and mauls their way out the door. Fresh air. Breathing room. Dylan releases my hand. We survived.

"Now you're a local," says Yuki's brother as his colossal hand smacks my back.

The Yomiuri Giants play at Tokyo Dome. As we approach the stadium, Haru stops me and points to a huge roller-coaster that looks like it's coming out of the stadium roof.

"It's called the Thunder Dolphin. We must come back another time and visit the amusement park," Haru says.

"An amusement park? In the stadium?" I ask.

"Right next door," Yuki says. "We'll come back when it's not so busy."

Haru nods in agreement, and they keep walking. Dylan and I stop and stare in amazement at the roller-coaster, wondering what other awesome rides are out there.

"Today, we watch baseball," says Yuki's brother, who gives us a little shove. He's a guy of few words, but he certainly gets his point across.

Yuki's dad takes us to a vendor inside the stadium to buy cheering toys. Haru and I choose a giant stick with a cartoon head and a clapper. Dylan picks out a towel with a player's name on it. He ties it around his head, but Yuki pulls it off and swings it around in the air. "You use the towel to cheer like this." Yuki chooses a pink stuffed tiger. Sometimes I forget she's a girl.

Next stop: food. Yuki's dad and brother line up to buy something called a "Dome Melon-pan," which is a pork sandwich on a sweet bun with honey mustard. It sounds pretty good, but Yuki insists that we choose from a giant poster with pictures of bento lined up next to smiling baseball players.

"Each player has their favourite bento. You can pick a player and get his favourite lunch," Yuki tells me and giggles a little.

Haru rolls his eyes and points at a Giants player next to something that looks like fried chicken. Yuki goes right to her favourite player and chooses his bento. I select something that looks like the Dome Melon-pan because, let's be honest, that's what I actually want to eat.

"Maybe they will serve Jacob's Ramen one of these days," Haru says as we head to our seats.

"Jacob's Ramen?" Yuki asks. Haru is busy explaining to Yuki in Japanese all about my ramen recipe when we reach our seats. She is laughing and smiling. I'm not sure if she is impressed with my ramen or with Haru.

We take our seats just in time for the game to begin. Top of the first. Yuki's brother is whispering to his dad in Japanese. My guess is he's sizing up the pitcher since I'm sizing up the second baseman.

The first pitch. Batter swings and misses. Strike. The second pitch. Way out of the box. Ball. The third pitch. Contact. Straight down the middle. Runner starts. The opposing crowd begins to cheer. The Giants fans are silent. The midfielder gets it. Quick toss to first base. Out. The Giants fans are now applauding. The moment the second batter appears, the crowd goes silent. Is this part of the harmony thing? No heckling? Strange.

I watch the pitcher closely. Three fastballs. Three strikes. Third batter. Three fastballs. Three strikes. Wow, that guy has an arm on him. The crowd breaks into some cheer as we move into the bottom of the inning.

"It's the Giants Cheer," Yuki yells to me over all the noise. It's deafening. Exciting. Every person in the crowd is cheering like it's the World Series. Yuki starts to sing along with Haru. Dylan and I clap and wave our toys around. I can make out a part where everyone yells, "Viva Giants," and then what sounds like a soccer chant: "*Oi oi oi.*"

The next five innings pretty much play out the same: fastballs and a few runs. The home team is quiet while the opposing team cheers and vice versa. At one point, a guy dressed like a sumo wrestler comes running out with a drum and pounds out the beat for the Giant's cheer. I am able to sing along—to most of it anyhow. At the top of the seventh, it's Home–5, Visitor–3. We head back for more food. This time, we eat ice cream out of little souvenir batting hats. I try to start a conversation with Yuki's brother.

"That pitcher throws a lot of fastballs," I offer.

"They aren't all fastballs. Some are Gyroballs," he says.

"What is that?" I ask.

"A uniquely Japanese pitch," he says. He pulls a ball out of his backpack and shows me. "It starts with a fastball grip, but it doesn't backspin. You need specific movements with your wrist and arm to almost make a knuckleball but with fastball speed," he explains.

"Wow, can you throw one?" I ask.

"I'm working on it," he says. "Do you play baseball?"

"Yeah, I play second base."

"Any good?"

I shrug. "I do alright. MVP at last year's tournament."

He nods his head in approval and hands the ball to me. "Next time, you come to watch my team."

"*Arigato*," I say and put the ball into my bag.

"Do you go to the international school too?" I ask.

"No, I go to a Japanese high school. It's the only way to play Japanese baseball and possibly enter the *Koshien*," he says.

"What's that? A tournament?" I ask.

"Yes, it's the biggest baseball tournament in Japan. Bigger than the professional leagues. Bigger than the Giants."

"Does the international school not have baseball teams?"

"They do, but they play other international schools."

This got me thinking. I could be playing baseball this fall.

"So you stay in the Japanese school hoping to be in this tournament?" I ask.

"Yeah," he responds.

"Wow, you must be good," I say.

"He's amazing!" Yuki says. "Maybe he can introduce you to some teams to practise with," she says with a pleading gaze at her brother.

"Sure, I'll ask around," he says.

"Thank you!" I say. I try not to sound too eager, but I can't wait to get back on the field.

By the time the game is over, my stomach is full, and my voice is hoarse. The Giants won. Yuki tells me the Giants always win. I might have to check some stats before believing that.

We hang around Tokyo Dome City for a bit after the game to avoid the subway crowds. On the ride home, Haru calls out to me from across the train, "Viva Giants," and a group of us chant back, "*Oi Oi Oi*." I look around at my new group of baseball and food-loving friends, and I feel right at home.

CHAPTER THIRTEEN

The Karuizawa Trip

"DAD, DO YOU think we could set up a pitch-back net on the balcony?"

"That doesn't sound very safe," Dad says without looking up from his phone.

"Why not?" I persist.

"How do you expect to recover the balls you miss?"

"I never miss."

"Right."

"Mom!" I yell upstairs, "Can I get a pitch-back net?"

"A what?!" she calls from upstairs.

"Never mind."

"Look, Jacob, we're leaving soon for our weekend trip to Karuizawa. Why don't you focus on packing?" Dad says.

"I packed three days ago," Lily brags as she enters the kitchen. "I read there are forests in Karuizawa. Actual forests!"

"And *onsen*," Dylan adds as he opens the fridge, searching for breakfast.

"Onsen? Isn't that just a hot spring?" I ask.

"Yeah, but you get to go in NAKED!" says Lily.

"What?" I ask.

"Naked," repeats Lily.

"Like a bath?" Dylan asks.

"Like a giant naked bath for the whole family," says Mom as she pushes past Dylan and pours a third cup of coffee.

"You mean we go in together?" I ask in horror.

"Yup," replies Mom.

"Hell, no!" is the only response Dylan can come up with.

"Language!" Mom warns.

I storm upstairs to hide in my bedroom and pack three pairs of swimming shorts. I'm thinking about a hack to survive this and am considering duct tape on my goggles, but instead, I text Haru.

"Haru?"

Nothing.

"Haru. It's an emergency."

"What is it?" he types.

"What is an onsen? Will I be naked with my family?"

"It's a hot spring bath. So yes," he replies.

This really is my worst nightmare.

"Can I wear a swimsuit?" I type.

"No."

"&*@**%^."

"It's fine. Everyone does it. Don't be a Chester."

"No way," I reply. "But good use of the word Chester."

"The whole family will be naked. Not just you," he types.

"So?"

"Everyone is the same. So no big deal," Haru replies.

He's right. Naked, helpless, in a pool of hot water. This could be an opportunity.

"Haru, *Arigato*," I reply.

"You are welcome," he texts.

"Jacob, are you packed yet?" Dad calls from downstairs.

"Yes, Dad! I have everything I need," I yell back. Everything. Absolutely everything.

● ● ●

"It's about two hours on the Shinkansen," Dad tells me as I settle into my seat. A Shinkansen is a bullet train that travels at 200 miles per hour—that's double the speed of the fastest pitch recorded. "When we get to Karuizawa, we can head straight for the onsen to relax," Dad continues.

"Awesome," I quickly reply.

"I thought you weren't going in the onsen," Dylan says.

I shrug. "I've come around."

"What about the hike?" Lily asks.

"We'll do the hike tomorrow," Dad says.

"Come on! Why do we always have to do what I want last . . ." Lily whines. "I never—"

Cue headphones. Music, check—two hours of peace.

● ● ●

"Put on your yukata and meet me in the lobby," Dad instructs as he ties his robe closed.

"I'm coming with you; I want to see the lobby flower arrangements," Mom says as she struggles to jam her large feet into the tiny hotel slippers and sneak out the hotel room door.

We are staying at a traditional Japanese hotel called a Ryokan. The rooms have tatami mats instead of carpet, and the people wear yukata instead of suits; paintings of samurai and sumi-e are on every wall. It is a far cry from Tokyo's modern conveniences, a step back in time to the old Japan my parents love so much.

"Do we have to wear a yukata?" I ask Dylan.

"Why not?" he asks as he ties his shut.

"Because we look like Dad on a Sunday morning," I say.

"So what?" asks Dylan.

"So if I don't tie this right, everyone in the lobby is going to see my nuts," I tell him.

"I'm ready," says Lily. She has put on her swim cap.

"This isn't a swim meet, Lily. It's like a hot tub," I tell her.

"Doesn't matter. This cap will keep my head warm."

"It's a thousand degrees outside, and you're basically in a hot tub. I think you'll be warm."

"It's my head. My decision," she insists.

"Whatever."

"What's in the bag?" she asks.

"Nothing. My goggles." I can't let them see my secret.

"I thought we weren't going underwater," Lily says.

"It's my head. My decision," I say.

"Whatever."

"Let's go," says Dylan as he pulls his yukata belt tighter. "I wanted to check out the sumi-e paintings in the lobby."

"Seriously?" I ask.

"Of course not. Sumi-e is lame. I quit," he says.

"How'd you get out of that?" I ask. There is no way Mom would just let him quit.

"When Mom found the nude manga that you hid in my top drawer, I told her that my sumi-e teacher gave it to me."

"Wow. Way to turn that around, dude," I say.

He looked at me funny. "Um, thanks."

"What did Mom do?" I ask.

"She called and yelled at my teacher for twenty minutes, but he doesn't speak English, so I doubt that went anywhere." He pulled at his robe. "Come on, let's go."

"I'll catch up," I say as I head into the bathroom and wait to hear the door close. I peek out of the hotel room and watch them get on the elevator. I run for the stairs and make a mad dash for the onsen. I jump the fence into the hot spring area and hide something in a bush near the water, then sneak back into the change rooms just as Dylan and Dad enter.

"How'd you get here so fast?" Dylan asked.

"I took the stairs," I say, trying to breathe normally and not sound like I've just run a marathon.

"Why?"

"Why not?"

Dylan is suspicious, so I change the topic. "So, Dad, we have to share the bath with the girls, but we get our own locker room?"

"Yes, it would appear so," Dad answers. Even he looks a little skeptical when he sees the showers: a tiny wooden stool, a tiny wooden cup, and a tiny tap.

"Where's the shower?" Dylan asks.

"I think that is the shower," Dad reluctantly answers. There is a sign with a picture of a person sitting on the tiny stool, naked, pouring water from the tap over his body.

"Wash up, boys," Dad instructs.

"But ..." Dylan starts.

"Just do it," Dad tells him. We sit on the stools and attempt to wash our bodies one cup at a time.

"Ok, let's go," Dylan says, holding the little facecloth we got upon entry.

"What am I supposed to do with this?" I ask, holding up my cloth. He shrugs. I put the little facecloth over my eyes so as not to see my naked mom and sister as we head towards the hot springs.

"Brilliant," says Dylan.

"All-Star Expat," I reply.

"What?"

"Nothing."

"Oh, look, there's a fence between the men and women," says Dad in relief.

"What?" I pull the face cloth off my face. Sure enough, there is a wooden barrier between the men's and women's hot springs.

"Oh, thank God," Dylan says.

"Girls, can you hear me?" calls Dad.

"Yes, we hear you," answers Mom.

A little waterfall on the far side of the hot spring is the perfect place to rest for a minute. The relief of having a wall between the men and women allows me to relax in the warm water and clear my mind and wait for Dylan's screams.

"AHHHHH!" yells Mom.

"What's going on?" calls Dad.

"AHHHHH! Get over here!"

"What's happening?" Dad asks.

"AHHH! SNAKE!"

"Did she say snake?" asks Dylan.

"Impossible," says Dad.

"Snake?" I say as I slowly come back to reality. Oh no! The rubber snake I'd left for Dylan was on the wrong side of the fence.

"SNAKE!!! GET OUT, LILY!" Mom shouts.

"What?"

"GET OUT!"

Within seconds, my naked mother and sister, complete with bathing caps, come running around the barrier, naked bodies jiggling as they run, private parts all out in the open, then leap into our onsen. Mom lands directly on Dylan.

"There was a snake in our water!" Mom yells.
"I didn't see a snake!" Lily replies.
"There was a snake!" says Mom.
Although I didn't get to see Dylan's reaction to a snake, the look on his face as my butt-naked mother jumped into the pool on top of him will give me laughs for years.

• • •

"Should we go for a dip in the Onsen before breakfast?" Dad asks the next morning. The drop-dead look from Mom is all the answer he needs. "OK, breakfast it is," he says.

At the Ryokan, everyone gets the same breakfast: rice, miso soup, grilled fish, pickled vegetables, and a boiled egg in a soy sauce soup. Looks great to me. My mom looks less than impressed.

"Could I have some toast, please?" she asks the server. The server doesn't understand.

"Just eat what's there," Dad whispers to Mom.

She clenches her teeth. "I don't want fish and pickles for breakfast. I want toast."

She is still angry about the snake and has decided it's all Dad's fault for bringing us to this Ryokan. I feel a little guilty watching Dad suffer. A little.

"Just eat the fish," Dad mumbles.

"You eat fish!" Mom pushes her bowl towards Dad.

"OK, OK, I think I know the word for bread." Dad says something to the server, who shakes her head. He repeats it. The server tilts her head to the side like a puppy who is learning a new trick. She shuffles away to the kitchen and returns with a frying pan. Dad looks at Dylan, Dylan to me, then Lily to Mom. Dad holds his breath.

"I'm done," is all Mom says, and she storms out of the restaurant.

"What did you ask for?" I question.

Dad shrugs. "The Japanese word for bread is 'pan.' I didn't think they would give me a pan."

"I think this trip is a little too authentic for Mom," I say.

"Eat your pickles, kids; we have a hike to do," Dad barks as he eats Mom's fish.

● ● ●

"Fresh air, just what we need," Dad says as we start our hike. No one responds. I haven't been to a real forest since we arrived in Japan, and it feels great to be surrounded by trees again, even if they are much shorter. Lily keeps running ahead and hiding. She is all over the place, searching for bugs and playing with sticks.

Dylan attempts to read the trail map we got at the Ryokan. "I think there is a temple if we hike to the top of the mountain—and maybe soup?" He turns the map around as if it's easier to read upside down.

Mom is silent and in an almost meditative state. My guess is that she's starving.

"Let me see." I take the map from him. At the top of the mountain path, there is an icon for a temple and an icon for a steaming bowl. That can only mean one thing—ramen.

"Let's get moving; there is ramen at the top of this mountain," I say.

Mom hears the word ramen and comes back to life. "Excellent!" she says and pushes past Dad to the front of the line. There is a purpose in our steps as we hike uphill, sweat dripping off our chins.

"What will we see at the temple?" Dylan asks between huffs.

"Not sure," Dad answers.

"Will we get to wash money?" I ask.

"No, not here," Dad says.

"What kind of temple is it then?" Dylan wonders aloud.

"I don't know." Dad pulls out his phone to look it up. He always wants to have the answers. "Sorry, no reception, kids." We keep hiking and finally see a clearing with a couple of small wooden houses. One of the houses has a steaming bowl of ramen painted on the side, and the other side has a small

Buddha statue and a bench for praying. There are a couple of monks out front working in the garden.

"That's the temple?" Dylan.

"I guess so," says Dad.

"Lily, why don't we go see about some lunch?" Mom asks. No reply.

"Lily?" she repeats. We all look around. There is no Lily.

"Lily! Get out of the bushes; we're here," Mom yells. The monks stop what they are doing and look up at us.

"Lily?" Dad says.

"Lily?" Dylan calls.

"Lily!" I yell. I go back into the forest. "Come out, Lily, we're here. Enough hiding." No response.

"Where is that impossible child?" Mom exclaims.

"Lily!" Dad shouts. One of the monks wanders over and, in broken English, asks if we are OK. Mom starts in about her frustrating daughter—who always spends more time paying attention to bugs under logs and worms climbing out of trees than to the actual world around her—and how she's not surprised that she got lost in the forest because she always gets lost in the woods. On and on and on.

"Mom, he doesn't understand you," I say.

"LILY!" Mom screams. I ask Dad for his phone; I show the monk a picture of Lily on it. I point to the forest and give all sorts of gestures that the monk seems to understand. The monk bows slightly and goes back to the other monk and, after a short conversation, puts on his straw hat, walks into the ramen shop, comes out with a small bag of stuff, and gestures for me to follow him into the forest.

"OK, I guess I'm going to look for Lily," I tell Dad. Dad starts to leave with us. The monk shakes his head and gestures the rest of the family towards the ramen shop. He points to me and the forest. Dad looks concerned.

"It's all right, Dad, we'll find her," I tell him. It's not the first time I have seen my dad worried, but he also looks defeated. This holiday is a bust, and he knows it.

The monk is quiet, but he keeps a good pace. He doesn't seem to be looking for Lily as much as he is heading somewhere. Now and then, I call out for Lily but no response. We reach a fork in the path, and the monk leads us left.

"*Sumimasen.* We came from this way." I point right down the hill. He waves his hand dismissively and starts left.

"But we didn't come this way," I repeat as I run to catch up.

"Lily!" I yell. The monk stops and motions for silence by putting his hand to his lips. For a brief moment, I wonder if this strange man is leading me into the forest for some other reason. What's in his bag? Firewood? A cauldron? Am I to be the next meal of the only living cannibalistic monk?

As we stand still in silence, I hear something in the distance. The monk starts to walk again, even more briskly, and I follow. The sound is louder now, and it's running water. The path stops, and we are at a small waterfall. Sure enough, there's Lily, sitting by the waterfall barefoot, splashing and poking at some frogs.

"Lily!" I run to her.

"Hi, Jacob. Look at this beautiful waterfall I found," she says, utterly oblivious as usual.

"Lily, seriously? Mom and Dad are flipping out!"

"Why?"

"Why? You ran away in the forest. Again."

"No, I didn't. I found the waterfall. What took you so long?"

"We weren't going to a waterfall; we were going to the temple."

"Well, I was heading to the waterfall," she says with a snarky tone and splashes her feet in the water. I wander in circles for a moment until I get reception and text Dad to tell him we are OK. The monk reaches into his bag and pulls out a thermos, some teacups, and a bag of dried apricots.

"Who is your friend?" Lily asks.

"He's not my friend; he's a monk who offered to help find you," I say.

"Well, he's setting up a picnic," Lily says. I try to explain to the monk that we have to get back before my mom loses it, but the monk doesn't budge. He is drinking his tea and offering the bag of apricots to me. I take an apricot and pop it in my mouth. The sweetness is good after all those pickles and eggs at breakfast. Mom and Dad can wait a few more minutes. The three of us drink tea, dip our toes in the water, and eat apricots. The monk points to a large rock on the other side of the water and says, "*Minogame.*"

"*Minogame?*" I don't know what that means.

"*Minogame,*" he repeats. He picks up a stick and starts to draw something in the dirt. I can't make it out.

"It's a turtle with a giant tail," Lily says, tilting her head to the side to get a better look.

"Hi, hi," says the monk. "Turtle, *kame.*"

"I think he thinks that rock looks like a turtle," says Lily. I look across the water to the rock again. It does look like a turtle with a huge tail.

"*Minogame,*" the monk repeats, pointing at the turtle. He clasps his hands together and bows his head. He stands there, praying in silence at the rock for a minute. Only in Japan would a turtle-looking rock be sacred.

Lily breaks the silence. "See, isn't this better than a temple?"

"Yeah," I reply and lean back to rest in the grass, "but I was looking forward to some ramen."

"Ramen?" Lily shrieks.

"Yes, there is a ramen restaurant by the temple," I reply and take a deep breath to relax.

"Ramen?!" Lily shrieks. She is putting on her shoes and tossing her tea into the water. She grabs my cup and the monk's cup too. She stuffs them into his bag and motions for him to get up and get moving.

"*Sumimasen*," I say to the monk. He laughs, puts on his slippers, and leads us back toward the temple.

That afternoon we visited museums and shopped for antiques. Mom spent enough money on odd-looking statues and tea ceremony junk that she was happy again. Dad got his confidence back when everyone loved his plan to eat cake and ice cream for dinner. That's the thing about family holidays—no matter how hard I try to hate them, there is always something that makes it worthwhile, like a secret waterfall, dessert for dinner, or scarring your brother for life with visions of his naked mother jumping on top of him.

CHAPTER FOURTEEN

Teamwork

HARU AND I are hanging out at the park, and I'm filling him in on the rubber snake in the *onsen* incident.

"So Dylan jumped right on top of your mom?" Haru asks.

"Amazing, right?!"

"Why are you so mean to your brother?"

"Because that's what brothers do."

"Dylan doesn't do that to you."

"Sure he does. Remember when he pushed me on the unicycle?"

"Not the same," he finishes.

We are quiet for a moment. I'm not in the mood for Haru's be-nice-to-everyone-harmony-as-one speech. He grabs his baseball and glove and walks over to an open space. I pick up my glove and join him. We start to play catch.

"I've got an even better story to tell you," I say. "Do you remember Dylan was taking sumi-e classes?"

"Yes. Why? Did he stop?"

"Yes, he stopped because his teacher gave him a nude manga, and my mom completely freaked out."

"That's terrible," Haru says. I knew he would say that.

"Wait until you hear the best part. The teacher didn't give it to him at all. I snuck it into his drawer, and when Mom found it, Dylan blamed his sumi-e teacher."

Haru misses the catch. "Wait, you put it there, and Dylan blamed the teacher? He did that to stop you from getting in trouble?" he asks.

"No. Dylan used the opportunity to get out of sumi-e." I start laughing. It was a brilliant play by Dylan.

Haru heads back to the benches and starts to pack up his stuff. "I thought Tokyo would change you, but it has not. You are a selfish person."

"Dylan's the one who blamed his teacher," I argue.

"But you did it! He only blamed his teacher because he didn't want to get you in trouble."

"No, that's not it. Come on, Haru. You don't think it's funny?"

"No. I would never allow someone to get in big trouble for something they didn't do. I am an honest person."

"You never ratted us out for breaking the water tap, did you? How honest were you then?" I argue.

"Maybe I should have," he says and storms off.

I'm steaming mad. Who is Haru to lecture me on what is right and wrong? When I get home, Dylan is gaming in our room. "I've had it with this country and all its better-than-you people," I say.

'What?" he says with his headphones still on.

"Argh!" I yell. He takes off his headphones and stops the game.

"What happened?" he asks.

"Haru says that it's all my fault that you got your sumi-e teacher in trouble."

"Well, you did put the manga in my drawer."

"But you blamed the teacher," I say.

"Would you rather I blamed you?" he asks.

It hit me like a wild pitch. Dylan didn't blame his sumi-e teacher, thinking that it would get him out of sumi-e. He blamed his teacher to protect me. Haru was right. Dylan was trying to help me out, and I was happy to watch the teacher get yelled at for no reason.

"So you never wanted to get out of sumi-e?" I ask.

"Well, no, well, yes. I don't know. It was pretty lame, but I feel bad that my teacher got in trouble. He was kind of cool."

"So I'm a jerk," I say.

"What? No."

"Ever since I moved here, it seems like no one can take a joke," I say.

"Maybe you're just trying too hard," Dylan responds.

"Trying too hard to what?"

"I don't know. Cause trouble. Make everyone unhappy. Let us know that you hate it here," Dylan says.

"But I don't hate it here. I actually like Japan," I say.

"Then act like it," he says, putting his headphones back on.

It was then I realized that maybe being straight with my family is a start towards understanding the whole Japanese harmony stuff. And if I can wrap my head around this "we-before-me" idea, then maybe I'll feel more at home.

If you thought the screaming was loud when Mom discovered the snake, you should have heard her when I told her the truth about the nude manga. So now, Dylan and I are stuck doing all sorts of chores and are being forced to apologize to the sumi-e teacher in person. Although I can't see that being too bad because, once again, the guy doesn't speak a word of English.

CHAPTER FIFTEEN

Karaoke

"HARU," I TEXT.

Nothing.

"Haru. I came clean. I'm going to be doing chores until I'm old. *Sumimasen.*" Long pause.

"*Gomen,*" he texts.

"What?"

"*Gomen.* That's how friends say sorry."

"So we are still friends?"

"Of course."

"*Gomen,*" I say.

"You know what we should do?" he texts.

"What?"

"Karaoke."

"Sure," I text back.

I can't say no after apologizing, but there is no way I am doing karaoke. I've done a pretty good job of staying away from all events that involve me singing. I even faked hand, foot, and mouth disease to get out of a school concert in second grade. I tried again in third grade, but I learned it's not that common of a disease. Should have gone with the flu.

I've done karaoke once—at a pool party for Dad's uncle, where the whole family rented a karaoke machine. A group of drunk adults, small children, a body of water, a chewed extension cord, blasting music, and a crazy uncle. What could have happened other than a complete and total disaster? The family has pretty much stayed clear of karaoke since, but you can't live in Tokyo and avoid it forever. It will find you.

Ten minutes later, Yuki texts me: "Friday. Akihabara. Karaoke."

"I'm busy," I respond.

"Doing what?" She knows I'm not busy.

"Something."

"What?"

"Anything."

"You're coming. Haru and I already planned it."

And that was it. Yuki is so bossy sometimes.

● ● ●

"I can't believe you've been in Tokyo this long and still haven't done karaoke," Haru says. We are walking to the subway on our way to karaoke in Akihabara.

"I hate singing."

"Nobody hates singing."

"Yes, I hate singing."

"Sing for me," he asks.

"I'm not going to sing for you."

He stops walking. "Practise. Here. Right now," he insists.

"Never going to happen."

"Listen," he says and starts singing "My Heart Will Go On."

"Hold on. Are you singing Celine Dion?" I ask.

"Yes, that is my favourite karaoke song, other than 'Lemon' by Kenzie Yonezu, but you won't know that one," he explains.

"Well, I don't know Celine Dion either," I say.

"But you guessed the song."

"Whatever. I am not singing right here in public," I say. He nods his head but looks concerned. Here we go again; Haru is worried that I'm going to stand out from the crowd by not participating and ruin the "peaceful harmony" of the group. It's a lot of work having to always worry about everyone's feelings and putting the group ahead of myself.

● ● ●

"You made it!" Yuki is overly excited to see us.

"We did," I reply.

"*Konichiwa*," Haru formally says hello.

"Hey!" Yuki replies.

I am happy to see that we aren't singing in a big open space but instead have a private room with snacks and a giant TV screen. There are two couches already crowded with a group of Yuki's friends I've never met. Haru is formally introducing himself to each of the girls and pointing at me. I'm not sure if he is introducing me or telling them that I'm afraid of singing. Whatever he's saying, they giggle each time he says it.

"Enough talking. More singing," Yuki demands. Three of the girls jump up as if on command and sing a Beatles song, entirely out of unison and off-key. Everyone claps.

The next performer sits on the couch and belts out a slow Japanese song. It must be a sad song because tears start dripping down her face halfway through. When she finishes the song, there is a silent pause while they all stop to think about whatever the heck she was singing about—a breakup, a lost dog, a broken bike. Who knows? I am starting to think I made a mistake coming here.

"Haru. Haru. Haru," they chant. He stands up, brushes the hair away from his face, pulls out his tucked-in T-shirt, and adjusts the microphone on the stand to the perfect height. My shy, reserved, little friend, who I thought would never even talk to a group of girls, is suddenly in his element. I swear I saw him wink at the teary-eyed one just before the music started. He sings his song, "Lemon," from the first line to the final note without a flinch, other than a slight quiver of his bottom lip, but I think that was for added effect.

The girls cheer wildly, and even I find myself clapping. He makes a quick bow, tucks his shirt back in, takes a drink from the fridge, and sits properly on the couch, back to his usual self.

Yuki goes next with some eighties power ballad I've heard Mom play while doing dishes. The rest of the girls work in groups or take turns. None of them come close to Haru's performance.

"I chose a song for you," Yuki tells me. "Get up; it's your turn."

"I'm OK."

"Everyone has to sing," Yuki says. There are twelve sets of eyes staring at me. Haru's are the most intense as they are narrowing, his brow stiffening. I see lines forming across his face. He is sending me a silent message: If I don't take part, I'll ruin it for everyone. This is my chance to prove to Haru that I can put the group before myself and that I can be respectful and fit in.

"OK, OK," I give in. "What is it?"

"You'll see." Yuki giggles.

The music kicks in. I recognize it immediately because Lily loves this song. It's "A Whole New World" from Disney's *Aladdin*. The first two lines come across the screen, and I watch intently, but no sound comes out of my mouth.

"Come on, Jacob, sing!" encourages Yuki. The next two lines pass. Suddenly, a voice kicks in. It's Haru, he's come to save me. He sings a few more lines and looks at me in anticipation.

I scan the room and see no one laughing or rolling their eyes. They are encouraging me, smiling, and singing along. I don't think they care how I may sound; they just want me to be part of the fun. I think I finally got it. It's like the team at the bottom of the league, who still play because they like the game. Even if some of the players suck, they always support each other. I lean into the mic and start singing.

Now I'm not saying we knocked it out of the park, but with Haru as my singing partner, we made it through, and for the first time in my life, I have a friend who I can trust to ultimately have my back, whether I strike out or have to sing princess songs to a group of girls. He will always put us ahead of him, and I think I finally get it.

"You don't totally suck! Well done, Jacob."

And then there is Yuki.

CHAPTER SIXTEEN

The Festival

THREE DAYS LEFT of summer vacation and then school starts. Yuki says I am already "more Japanese" than most of the kids who go to our school. Haru believes that after one year, I will be begging to come to his Japanese school because "the food is better, and the floors are clean." I can't wait to join the baseball team.

"Are you ready for the festival tonight?" Mom asks from behind the open fridge.

"I hope so. I've been cooking with Haru and Obaasan for a week straight," I say.

"I am so proud of you for helping Haru's family with their ramen booth," she says. "I am proud of how far you've come this summer."

"Come from where?" I ask.

"From hating this move to being part of the community," she says.

"Sure, Mom."

"I hear there are lots of games and prizes at the festival," Lily says.

"And music," Dylan adds.

"Yes, the Obon Festival is huge. Haru says our little neighbourhood is the place to be," I tell them. I offered to help Haru's family at their ramen stand because I've gotten pretty good at slicing and dicing under the watchful eye of Obaasan, and it gives me the chance to be close to the action.

"I'm off to help set up; see you there," I call out.

"See you there," Mom calls back. Tokyo may be the biggest city in the world, but it's also one of the safest. Mom has chilled out since we moved here and lets me go out on my own. Thinking back, every person I thought evil was just trying to help me—Haru, at the park, the guy on the train, the monk in the woods. I thought Canadians were the nicest people in the world, but I'm starting to think it might be the Japanese.

Another thing I've learned is that the Japanese love festivals. Haru has told me about so many festivals I can't keep track, but this one, the Obon Festival, is the biggest in our neighbourhood. It is a Buddhist festival called The Festival of Souls. It sounds creepy, but it means you celebrate family, dead and alive, like the Day of the Dead in Mexico. Haru tells me there are giant drums called taiko, music, dancing, food, games, and firecrackers. Everything needed for an awesome party.

"Jacob san. *Hayaku!*" Obaasan is calling me to hurry. I'm chopping green onions again. How fast does this woman want me to cut?

"No, Jacob. Not the onions. Obaasan wants to show you something." Haru takes the knife from my hand and places it next to the onions. He hands me a clean towel to wrap around my head and motions for me to follow him and Obaasan.

"*Miru*, look," says Obaasan. She points at a giant stage with a taiko drum where kids are lining up to give it a try.

"Oh, I don't know," I say. "Do I have to sing?"

"No singing, Jacob; this is a one-time chance," Haru says. "You must try." He pushes me towards the lineup, and I stand behind a small girl in a pink kimono. The little girl heads on stage. The drum is three times her size. A man wearing nothing but a cloth diaper and the same towel I have wrapped around my head hands her two giant sticks. He lines her up next to the drum, and she starts whacking it, one stick at a time, in a circular motion. After twenty hits or so, she steps back, bows, and hands the sticks to the man.

My turn. I freeze for a moment. Please don't let this be like karaoke! I climb the steps onto the stage and bow to the half-naked man, who smiles and hands me the sticks.

"*Arigato*," I say. He smiles again and gently shoves me into position. The flash of a camera blinds me. My family has found me.

"Go, Jacob!" Lily yells.

"Woohoo!" Dylan calls out.

"You got this, baby!" Mom yells as Dad takes another picture.

I try not to drop the sticks as I die of embarrassment. The man shoves me a little closer, encouraging me to start. I strike the drum. I can feel my feet vibrate, my heart pounding, my face blushing. The strong smell of bamboo and sweat is all around me. I hit the drum again. The man yells something and starts pounding on the drum beside me. I watch as he places his feet farther apart to brace himself like a batter getting ready for a pitch. I follow his lead and change my stance.

He yells something again, which sounds more like a chant. I try to match his tempo and keep striking the drum.

Boom bah boom. Boom boom bah bah boom. He stops hitting the drum and instead is hitting his sticks together while I keep on the drum. *Boom boom bah bah boom. Boom boom bah bah boom.* I can feel the drumming in my arms, my chest, and my toes. After another twenty hits or so, he stops and yells something that sounds like a finish. I look up from the drum to his face. He is smiling ear to ear, and I notice everyone around us is clapping and cheering. He bows to me and me to him. He pats me on my matching towel head and gives me a thumbs up. I bow again and climb back down the stairs.

"Sugoi!" Haru calls to me as he pushes through the crowd to join me.

"Thank you," I say. "That was awesome. Where can I learn to do that?" I ask.

"I know a place," Haru says in a serious tone. Now I know he won't rest until I am a taiko drummer. Haru doesn't take any request lightly.

"Haru san, Jacob san." Obaasan is pointing towards the ramen stand. Haru says something to her, they talk for a minute, and then he hugs her. I have never seen Haru hug his grandmother before, but he tells me that we have one hour of free time to check out the festival before Obaasan puts us to work.

Haru and I make our first stop at a stand selling *ramune*.

"This is a popular festival drink," Haru tells me.

"Why?"

"Watch," he says. The drink comes in a glass bottle with a marble at the top in place of a bottle cap. He buys two bottles, pulls them out of a giant bucket of ice, hands one to me, and then shows me how to open it. He pushes the marble into the glass bottle with his thumb, and the drink sprays out the top, dripping all over his hands and the ground. I follow his lead. It's icy cold, very bubbly, and has a lemon-lime flavour.

"*Blah, ramune,*" scoffs a voice behind me. "Festivals aren't about the drinks. They are about food!" It's Yuki.

"Yuki, you made it," I say.

"Of course," she replies and then says something to Haru in Japanese.

"Yes!" Haru replies.

"What?" I ask. Give it another year, and these two won't be able to talk behind my back.

"*Takoyaki,*" says Yuki. "That's what we need to eat. Right now."

Haru nods in agreement. I follow them to a stand selling what looks like balls of pancakes. I've been in Japan long enough to know there is no way they are simply pancakes with syrup. Sure enough, they're octopus pancake balls covered in a sweet ketchup-like sauce. Not bad. We then jump over to a stand selling BBQ corn with a teriyaki sauce on it. Haru eats two of them. Next, we find some sweet, sticky rice cakes filled with red bean curd. I eat three. Just when I think my stomach is going to explode, Yuki and Haru suggest some *yakisoba.*

"No more food. Let's try some games," I suggest.

"Let's go try the *kame* game," says Haru. We have to fight off a crowd of kids to get to the front of the game, and there is Lily.

"Just one more!" she is begging my mom.

"Three is enough, Lily," Mom tells her.

"But they are so cute, Mommy," she whines. I look over to see what she has, and sure enough, they are turtles. Of course, *kame,* the word for turtle. The kids are winning live baby turtles. Lily is holding three plastic bags, each filled with an inch of water and a tiny turtle. I watch the next boy play.

He is given a plain ice cream cone with a clothespin attached to it. He dips the cone into the water and is trying to catch one of the baby turtles swimming in the pool before his cone gets soggy and falls off the clothespin. Lily spots me.

"Jacob, Jacob, you have to catch me more baby turtles," she yells. She has a glimmer in her eye, and her hand is twitching. I haven't seen her this excited since she snuck that cicada into the house.

I give the attendant my money, and she gives me a cone. I hold on to the clothespin and start fishing. It gets soggy very fast and drops into the water.

"Try again," says Yuki, and she pays for me. This time, I locate a baby turtle before dipping my cone. I dive in quickly and catch the little guy right away. I see it struggling and trying to climb out of the cone. I pull it out and put the cone under my hand before it falls off.

"*Yatta*! I did it!" I call out.

Lily pushes around the pool, trying to get to me.

"No, Lily, it's mine," I tell her as the attendant hands the bagged turtle to me.

"Fine," says Lily with a huff, and she and Mom walk away.

"We better get to work," Haru says, and we wave goodbye to Yuki.

"I will see you at school on Monday," she replies, "You're going to love it." She gives Haru and me a quick hug and disappears into the crowd.

"Do you think Yuki would go on a date with me?" Haru asks me.

"Absolutely," I say, and I won't rest until he gets the courage to ask her out. I don't take Haru's requests lightly either.

Obaasan seems unimpressed with my new pet, but she finds a safe spot for it beneath the extra soup bowls. I have every intention of setting my baby turtle free near the pond on my way home. I just hope it doesn't get cooked into a soup before then. The next few hours are a total blur. I am working so hard to chop, stir, pour, serve, and use all of the Japanese words I know and keep them straight. I am knee-deep in hot soup when I hear an American voice in front of me.

"Excuse me."

"Irasshaimase," I reply automatically.

"Excuse me," he repeats. I look up. It is the two boys from the grocery store who were playing catch with the fruit.

"Oh, hello," I reply.

"Are you that kid from the grocery store?" he asks me.

"Yeah."

"I'm Carter. This is my brother, Cameron." He points to the other guy.

"I'm Jacob." I reach out my hand to shake theirs. There is an awkward pause.

"Sorry we bothered you and your friend at the store," Carter says.

I shrug. "That's OK."

"We're new to Tokyo," he says, "and things are different here."

I'm not sure why he would think throwing fruit in a store would be OK in any culture, but I'm in a good mood, so I give him the benefit of the doubt. Gaijins can be pretty stupid sometimes.

"Jacob san. Boru *onegaishimasu*," barks Obaasan. She is holding her hand out for a bowl.

"*Sumimasen*, Obaasan, *boru*," I reply, bow slightly, and hand her a bowl.

"How long have you lived in Tokyo?" asks Cameron.

"Three months," I reply. They look at me in shock.

"We saw you on stage playing the drum," says Carter.

"And you speak Japanese," says Cameron.

"Barely," I reply and laugh a little. Haru rolls his eyes and smiles.

"Three months?" Carter asks.

"Yeah."

Let's do a reality check here: I'm working at a ramen booth, taking directions in Japanese. I have a towel wrapped around my head and just played the taiko drum on stage. My favourite food is ramen . . . and pizza. I love the Yomiuri Giants. I hate karaoke. My two best friends are Japanese, and I just won a new pet that I intend to set free because turtles are sacred animals. Yuki's right; I may be more Japanese than I think.

Have I successfully become an All-Star Expat? Does that mean it's time to go back to Seattle? Because I want to stay.

"Are you going to the international school up the road?" asks Carter.

"Yes," I reply as I chop some mushrooms.

"Me too; will you join the baseball team?" asks Carter.

"Definitely."

"Me too," says Carter. "I'll see you Monday?"

"See you Monday," I reply. He pays Haru for his ramen and looks inside the container suspiciously. "Is that an eraser?" he asks, pulling out the *naruto*.

"No, it's fish," I tell him with a laugh. He shrugs his shoulders and pops it in his mouth. There may be hope for this kid yet.

The Festival

Glossary of Japanese Words

In order of appearance in the book:

Manga: Japanese comic book

Konbanwa: Good evening

Ohayo Gozaimasu: Good morning

Sumimasen: Excuse me or I'm Sorry

Sugoi: Awesome

Irasshaimase: Welcome

Naruto: A cured fish found in ramen. Also the name of a manga series.

Hi: Yes

Obaasan: Grandmother

Gaijin: Foreigner

Hajimemashite: Nice to meet you

Tsuku-tsuku boshi: Sound a cicada makes

Anime: Japanese cartoon

Totoro: A popular Japanese anime character

Ah-so: I see

1–10: 1 Ichi, 2 Ni, 3 San, 4 Yon/Shi, 5 Go, 6 Rok, 7 Nana/Shichi, 8 Hatchi, 9 Kyuu, 10 Juu

Sumi-e: Brushed ink painting

Ohayo: Morning (informal)

Ikimashou Let's go

Kombu: Kelp

Umami: Popular Japanese savoury flavour

Katsuobushi: Dried, fermented, smoked tuna

Tare: The seasoning of the ramen

Dewa Mata Ashita: Well, see you tomorrow

Oishi: Delicious

Koshien: A popular Japanese amateur baseball tournament

Minogame: Ancient mythical turtle

Gomen: Sorry (informal)

Hayaku: Hurry up

Miru: Look

Taiko: Drum

Ramune: Fizzy drink

Takoyaki: Ball-shaped octopus pancake

Onegaishimasu: Please (formal)

About the Author

Brenda Cohen is the author of *Trading Pizza for Ramen* and a mother, wife, and businesswoman.

Having always wanted to be a writer, Brenda built a successful career as a copywriter, creative director, and marketing professional. Her favourite job, however, is the one she has right now: writing children's books and being the CMO of her own company, Award Pool, which she founded with her husband, Reuven, and their three kids.

When she's not writing, Brenda spends her time cooking with her kids, snuggling with her dog, practising Japanese, or painting abstract art. She is as comfortable starting a campfire in the backwoods of British Columbia as she is navigating the busy streets of Tokyo.

Brenda lives by the motto "You'll never regret being kind" and believes a walk in the forest can solve both writing blocks and dampened spirits.

Brenda is a proud Third Culture Kid (TCK), having grown up in Tokyo. She works hard to bring multiculturalism into everything she does.

Honest and creative, Brenda works hard to make the world a little better for everyone around her.

Connect with Brenda at
www.vagabondpoet.com

Want more from
Trading Pizza for Ramen?

You've read the book. Now take the next step in the adventure. Here are a few ways to explore and learn more:

Endless Adventures: From shrines to forests, arcades to onsens, ramen shops to baseball games, discover Japan!

New Language/New Words: Practice the Japanese words you've learned. See the glossary or visit vagabondpoet.com for more.

Collect Trading Cards and NFT: Visit vagabondpoet.com and collect *Trading Pizza for Ramen* character and location cards.

Discover Hidden Adventures: Visit vagabondpoet.com to discover hidden stories and narrations from Jacob.

Connect with the Expat Community:

As a Third Culture Kid, I know firsthand the struggles Jacob and his family experience. My family relocated to Tokyo when I was seven, and I spent thirteen years making Japan my home. *Trading Pizza for Ramen* reflects my struggles with living in a foreign country as well as my appreciation of Japanese culture. If you're struggling with a recent move and need someone to talk to, visit vagabondpoet.com for expat and relocation resources.

It's a big world out there! Keep exploring.

BLOCKCHAIN
VERIFIED IP

CPSIA information can be obtained
at www.ICGtesting.com
Printed in the USA
BVHW031246051022
648685BV00006B/169